THE SCHOOL YEAR
WAS ALMOST OVER . . .

Jana clasped her yearbook, looking at it through misty eyes. She ran her hand across the red-and-gold padded cover, wishing this year would never end. All around the table her friends were opening their yearbooks and pointing to pictures as they flipped the pages.

"Oh, look!" cried Melanie. "There's a shot of the cheerleaders, leading yells at the soap game. Oh, yuck! I look awful!"

"What do you mean, *you* look awful?" countered Beth. "Here's one of me as the witch in the Halloween show. Talk about awful! Look at that wart on my nose."

"Who's going to sign my book first?" cried Katie, holding a pen up in the air.

Memories flashed in each girl's mind. This year in seventh grade had been a very special time for all the members of The Fabulous Five—it was a year that none of them would ever forget. . . .

Bantam Skylark Books by Betty Haynes
Ask your bookseller for the books you have missed

THE FABULOUS FIVE

Yearbook Memories

BETSY HAYNES

A BANTAM SKYLARK BOOK®
NEW YORK • TORONTO • LONDON • SYDNEY • AUCKLAND

RL 5, 009–012

YEARBOOK MEMORIES

A Bantam Skylark Book / July 1992

*Skylark Books is a registered trademark of Bantam Books,
a division of Bantam Doubleday Dell Publishing Group, Inc.
Registered in U.S. Patent and Trademark Office and elsewhere.*

*The Fabulous Five is a registered trademark of Betsy Haynes
and James Haynes*

ISBN 0-553-15975-5

Published simultaneously in the United States and Canada

*Bantam Books are published by Bantam Books, a division of Bantam Doubleday
Dell Publishing Group, Inc. Its trademark, consisting of the words "Bantam
Books" and the portrayal of a rooster, is Registered in U.S. Patent and Trade-
mark Office and in other countries. Marca Registrada. Bantam Books, 666 Fifth
Avenue, New York, New York 10103.*

PRINTED IN THE UNITED STATES OF AMERICA

CWO   0   9   8   7   6   5   4   3   2   1

With special thanks to
Barbara Rosenblum and Ann Schwartz

Yearbook Memories

CHAPTER

1

"Oh, Randy, I'm so nervous," said Jana Morgan as she and her boyfriend, Randy Kirwan, walked through the corridors of Wakeman Junior High. They were headed toward the gymnasium, where the biggest party of the year, the Wakeman Junior High dinner-dance, marking the end of the school year, was about to begin.

Randy gave her a crooked smile. "What's to be nervous about? Afraid I'll smash your toes on the dance floor?"

Jana looked up at him and grinned. "No, silly. It's just that our first year at Wacko is over, and next year, when the school becomes Wakeman Middle School, everything is going to be *so* different. Instead of being the babies of Wacko, we're going

1

to be the oldest, the ones the younger kids will look up to."

"Is that what's making you nervous?" asked Randy.

"No, not really," Jana replied wistfully. "I guess it's just sort of sad for such a terrific year to be ending, and I'm sure tonight is going to be filled with lots of special memories."

"Yeah," agreed Randy. "We had some pretty great times."

"Jana! Randy! Wait up!"

Jana turned around to see Melanie Edwards and Shane Arrington hurrying toward them. She caught her breath. Like Randy, Shane was wearing a jacket and tie, but it was Melanie who drew her attention. Her party dress was royal blue velvet, and it fit tightly at the waist, flaring at the hips.

"Wow, Mel, you look terrific," called Jana.

"So do you," said Melanie.

Jana glanced down proudly at her own dress. It was pale blue and strapless, and the full organza skirt swung as she walked. "Thanks," she said.

"Have you seen the rest of The Fabulous Five?" asked Melanie.

"Not yet," said Jana. "But the first ones in the gym are supposed to hold a table."

When Randy and Shane opened the heavy double doors to the gym, Jana and Melanie stopped and stared inside in amazement. The cavernous room had been transformed into a wonderland of light and color. Laser lights flashed, and neon light-sticks in geometric patterns glowed in every dazzling color in the spectrum. Tables lined the far end of the room, and on one side of the stage Crazy Reggie Robards, the disc jockey on the local rock radio station, was already playing CDs. On the other side of the stage was the podium, where the principal, Mr. Bell, would present the awards and recognize student activities.

"Pretty good job, if I do say so myself," remarked Shane, grinning. Shane had been chairman of the committee that decorated the gym.

"Oh, Shane, it's wonderful!" Melanie gushed.

Suddenly Jana spotted Beth Barry. She was wearing a short, red-sequined tank dress and was waving madly from a table near the dance floor. Katie Shannon and Tony Calcaterra were with her, and so were Dekeisha Adams and Marcie Bee, who, like Beth, did not have dates for the evening.

When they had all found their places at the table, Jana leaned across to Katie and said, "Hey, I like your dress. The green with silver lamé really sets off your red hair."

Katie smiled appreciatively and replied, "Thanks, but did you get a load of what Tony's wearing?"

Jana looked puzzled. Tony had on a coat and tie, just like all the boys at the party. "What do you mean?"

"His earring." Katie pointed to the small gold stud in his left ear. "He's finally getting to wear it to a school function!"

Tony bowed low, laughing along with everyone else.

"I just wish Christie were here," said Beth, referring to Christie Winchell, the fifth member of The Fab Five, who had moved to London in the middle of the school year.

"We'll see her soon," assured Melanie. "She'll be home in just a few weeks, remember?"

Beth nodded sadly. "But she should be here tonight. She was a big part of our wonderful year."

"I'll bet she's thinking about us right now," added Jana, getting a faraway look in her eyes.

The waiters began serving the dinner of baked chicken and stuffing. No one said much while they ate. Everyone was thinking about the past year, while Crazy Reggie played all the popular songs they had listened to on the old Wurlitzer jukebox at Bumpers, the fast-food place where Wakeman students spent some of their free time together.

Dessert was brownie sundaes, and just as Jana was too stuffed to eat another bite, pushing her dessert plate away, Mr. Bell stepped up to the podium and turned on his microphone. Crazy Reggie took his cue and let the music slowly fade away.

"Good evening, boys and girls," Mr. Bell began. He was smiling broadly, and the bald spot on the top of his head reflected a rainbow of color. "I would like to welcome all of you to the last school function of the year, the Wakeman Junior High dinner-dance."

Applause rang out in the gym, and the principal waited for it to die away before speaking again.

"We will be recognizing student achievement in a few minutes, but first I'd like for our faculty to move among the tables and distribute your own personal copies of *The Wigwam*, this year's Wakeman yearbook."

There was more applause and lots of excited chatter as the teachers handed out yearbooks.

Jana clasped hers, looking at it through misty eyes. As the seventh-grade coeditors, she and Funny Hawthorne had worked long and hard. She ran her hand across the red-and-gold padded cover, wishing this year would never end.

"The yearbook is beautiful, Jana," said Melanie. "Just beautiful."

"Thanks," said Jana, smiling again. "But after all that work, I expected it to be as thick as a New York City telephone book!"

All around the table her friends were opening their yearbooks and pointing to pictures as they flipped the pages.

"Oh, look!" cried Melanie. "There's a shot of the cheerleaders, leading yells at the soap game. Oh, yuck! I look awful!"

"What do you mean, *you* look awful?" countered Beth. "Here's one of me as the witch in the Halloween show. Talk about awful! Look at that wart on my nose."

"Here's me and my buddy, Igor," said Shane, pointing proudly to a picture of him leaning against the school building with his pet iguana on his shoulder.

"Who's going to sign my book first?" cried Katie, holding a pen up in the air.

Jana listened to the chatter all around her as memories flashed in her mind of the good times she'd had working on the yearbook with Funny. Every assignment had been a challenge. But now that she thought about it, one assignment had almost ended in disaster. It was the time when Mr. Neal, the faculty advisor for *The Wigwam*, asked her to do a special full-page feature on the worst enemy of her life. . . .

JANA'S MEMORY

Everyone else was gone from the yearbook room, and I was putting on my jacket and gathering my books one afternoon after school, when Mr. Neal called me up to his desk. It always made me a little nervous to talk to Mr. Neal alone, since I had had a tremendous crush on him when he was my fifth-grade teacher at Mark Twain Elementary, but I took a deep breath and went up, anyway.

Dreamy Mr. Neal flashed me a dazzling smile and said, "Jana, I'd like to give you a very special assignment, if you have time to do it."

Even though I had been going steady with Randy Kirwan for more than a year, wild horses couldn't have kept me from accepting an assignment if Mr. Neal wanted me to have it. A very special assignment, he had called it. I could hardly wait to hear what it was.

"Sure, Mr. Neal. I'd be glad to," I said. I was surprised at how casual I sounded.

"Great," he replied, almost knocking me over with another one of those smiles. "Pull up a chair, and we'll talk about it."

As I pulled up a chair, I got a faint whiff of his cologne. It was heavenly. How was I going to look him in the eye without blushing?

"What I had in mind . . ." he began, leaning closer so that I was engulfed in Wild Man or Macho Musk or some other absolutely fabulous scent. I tried to think about Randy. Maybe I would buy him a bottle of dreamy Mr. Neal's cologne for Christmas. ". . . was a full-page feature on Wakeman's very own movie star, Taffy Sinclair."

Those last two words jolted me to attention. I blinked at him in disbelief. I knew I had a weird expression on my face—it probably looked as if I'd just thrown up. In another minute, I thought, I might. That's how sickening the idea was.

"Taffy Sinclair?" I murmured.

"Yes," said Mr. Neal. "You both went to the same elementary school, so you know her better than Funny does. Of course I remember that you didn't get along very well back then, but I'm sure you and Taffy have both matured a great deal."

It took all the effort I had to smile and nod. That we didn't get along back then was an understatement, if I ever heard one. He was right about our maturing, though. We had stopped waging war against each other a long time ago. We even said hello once in a while, but the idea that *I* would do a full-page feature on *her* was above and beyond the call of duty. She had made a television movie in Hollywood, and I was still . . . just plain Jana.

"Now I'd like for you to interview her," he went on, totally oblivious to my misery. "You know, ask her about life on the set, what famous movie stars she knows, things like that. And don't forget pictures. You should get some good shots of her yourself, but don't forget to ask her for any she might have brought back from Hollywood. This is Thursday." He paused, looking me straight in the eyes. "Do you think you can do the interview, take some shots, and show me a couple of layouts by Monday?"

Getting up to leave, I nodded, aware that I couldn't smell his cologne anymore. Misery had stopped up my nose.

When I got to Bumpers, my friends were still there. I slid into the booth with them and exploded, "You'll never guess what I have to do!"

They looked at me with astonishment when I explained.

"You're kidding," said Beth. "How could he ask such a thing."

"He thinks we've matured," I explained, rolling my eyes.

"Well, haven't you?" asked Katie. "I mean, it's been a long time since you two have actually had any problems."

I sighed. "Yeah, but . . ."

Even though Taffy had always hated all of The Fab Five, *I* had been her special enemy. It was *my* notebook she had gotten hold of when we had The Against Taffy Sinclair Club in fifth grade. And it was *me* she had blackmailed in sixth and *me* she had forced to carry her tray in the cafeteria. And it was *my* boyfriend, Randy Kirwan, she had tried over and over to steal. So what if we had matured? How could I ever forget all that?

When I got home, I stared at the telephone as if it were about to reach out and grab me. I knew I had to call Taffy and ask for an interview, but I also knew that I would have to swallow an awful lot of pride to do it.

I'll do it later, I thought. She's probably not home.

I didn't do it later. All evening, every time I looked at the phone, I thought of another excuse to put it off. And when I got to school the next morning and saw her talking to Alexis Duvall, I put it off again. They were probably having an important conversation. I didn't want to interrupt.

I was amazed on Friday at how many times I came in contact with Taffy Sinclair during the course of the day. Every time I rounded a corner in the halls, there she was—strutting along and acting like a big-deal movie star. I had even heard that she might get to star in a television series based on the movie she had made. I dreaded interviewing her more with each minute that went by.

Finally I couldn't put it off any longer. I absolutely couldn't face Mr. Neal on Monday without a layout—*dreamy* Mr. Neal and his fabulous cologne.

It was ten o'clock Saturday morning when I finally called her house. As soon as the phone began to ring, I cringed. Did movie stars get up as early as normal people? I had been up only half an hour myself, but maybe she slept till noon.

She answered the phone. "Hello. Sinclair residence, Taffy speaking," she said in a nauseatingly cheerful voice.

This was it. I took a deep breath. "Hi, Taffy. This is Jana."

"Oh, hi, Jana." Her voice registered total surprise.

There was no use keeping her in suspense. "Mr. Neal wants me to interview you this weekend so that we can do a special feature page on you in the yearbook. You know, since you're a movie star and everything. I was wondering if we could get together sometime."

"Oh, neat," she chirped. "Why don't you come over after lunch. I can show you all my souvenirs of Hollywood."

"Okay," I agreed, groaning to myself. "I'll see you about one o'clock."

After we hung up, I paced the floor, wondering how I was going to pull this off. But my training on the yearbook staff kicked in just then, and I sat down and made a list of things to ask her. I would keep the interview short and to the point. Take a few pictures and leave. Get out of there as fast as I could.

* * *

"Oh, Jana. I'm so glad you could come over," Taffy gushed when she opened the door. *Naturally* she looked terrific. Her long, blond hair was held back on each side by combs covered with ribbons the exact same shade of peach as her sweater. She was also wearing white jeans and white sneakers with peach-colored laces. And *naturally* her fingernail polish matched.

I felt like a dweeb in my faded blue jeans and red Wakeman sweatshirt with the pizza sauce stain on the front. The sweatshirt had been clean when I put it on this morning, but I'd had leftover pepperoni, mushroom, and green pepper pizza for lunch, and of course I'd missed my mouth. It had been too late to change, but now I wished I'd changed, anyway.

I followed Taffy through the house on tiptoes, feeling as if I were in a museum. Taffy's mother had been a member of the Radio City Music Hall Rockettes when she was young, and there were pictures everywhere of Mrs. Sinclair, who went by the stage name of Sally Starre, with famous musicians and movie stars. As I glanced around, I remembered thinking more than once that it probably explained why Taffy's mother pushed her so hard to succeed in show business. I certainly didn't envy Taffy for having a mother like that.

But if I thought all of this looked like a museum, it was nothing compared with her room. Even though I'd been there before, I couldn't help gawking when we stepped into the huge bedroom, decorated in all white. The walls, the carpet, the silk-draped canopy bed, it looked like a room out of a movie. Still, there was something different about Taffy's room since I'd last been there. It was Taffy's Hollywood souvenirs.

Photographs, posters, and newspaper clippings covered just about every square inch of the walls, and on her desk was a black-and-white clap-board with white chalk letters that read, NOBODY LIKES TIFFANY STAFFORD, SCENE #1, TAKE #1. As I looked around the room I couldn't help noticing that one face appeared with Taffy's in almost every picture. It was Raven Blaine, who was only the biggest teen idol in the world, and beside her bed sat a portrait of Raven, autographed: "To Taffy with Love. Raven."

As I stood there staring, I could see Taffy out of the corner of my eye, gloating, obviously eating up the chance to show off.

"That's Raven Blaine. You must have heard of him," she said, as if even a nobody like me couldn't miss knowing who Raven Blaine was.

"Yeah, I've heard of him," I mumbled.

She grabbed a photo album and flipped it open, patting a spot on the bed for me to sit beside her. "And here we are at the beach." She pointed to a picture of herself sitting on a blanket in an incredible blue bikini with Raven Blaine beside her, looking even more handsome than he did on the screen. "Sometimes he had to wear a red wig to disguise himself so that he wouldn't be mobbed by fans," she said, giggling.

My face felt as if it were made of cement. I couldn't smile. I probably wouldn't be able to move my lips to ask questions, either. I would only be able to sit there like a lump and try to imagine how it felt to be beautiful Taffy Sinclair on a California beach with handsome Raven Blaine.

I had a momentary flash of the old days, when we had been rivals at everything. One thing was certain now. We would never be rivals again. Not at anything. Taffy Sinclair had left me in her dust.

"Mr. Neal wanted me to ask you if you have any pictures from Hollywood that you'd like included in the layout," I managed to get out.

"Wow, yes," replied Taffy. "But not the bikini one." She flipped through the album and stopped at a series of pictures that had obviously been shot on the set of her movie. "Here. How about this one?" she asked, pointing to a shot of herself and—of course—Raven Blaine. They were standing in front of a school building and were wearing normal clothes. "Or this one." This time she was in the picture with Raven Blaine and a red-haired girl who looked vaguely familiar. "You know her, don't you? She's Paige Kramer. She used to star in *Daddy's Little Darling*. We became best friends while I was in Hollywood."

Of course I knew who Paige Kramer was, now that she mentioned it. Another child star! Probably as big a brat as Taffy Sinclair! I smiled weakly and took the picture of Taffy, Raven, and Paige. "You'll get this back," I murmured.

"You can have more if you want. Here. Take the whole album," she offered, pushing it toward me. "There are all sorts of interesting pictures in there."

I took the album and put it down on the bed beside me. Then I made the mistake of looking down at my shoes. My white leather sneakers were scratched and dingy, but beside them, Taffy's sneakers with the peach-color laces were gleaming white. They were so white, they were almost blinding. It was just one more example of how she was better than me.

"Did you say you wanted to ask me some questions?" Taffy asked.

"Oh, yeah." I fumbled around for my notebook, which was on the bed beside me, and scratched my ballpoint pen on the first page until a line of ink finally appeared.

Clearing my throat, I asked the first question. "How did it feel to leave home and go to Hollywood to star in a movie?"

"It was the biggest thrill of my life," answered Taffy, bouncing with excitement. "And the studio took terrific care of Mother and me. We had our own chauffeur-driven limousine, and everyone on the set was wonderful. I even had a *star* on my trailer door."

What an ego, I thought as I scribbled down her words. *It was the biggest thrill of my life . . . I even had a star on my door!* I mimicked her in my mind. I sat there, frowning and blacking out all the *o*'s in what I had just written while I waited for her to go on.

"And of course meeting Raven Blaine was the biggest thrill of all," she cried. "Did I show you the necklace he gave me?"

Of course she hadn't. I shook my head as she jumped up and danced over to her bureau, pulling a small jewelry box out of the top drawer. Then she dashed back to me and popped the box open right under my nose.

"Isn't it beautiful?"

I blinked at the gleaming gold star that hung from a delicate gold chain. Engraved on the star was a single word: TAFFY.

"That's nice," I said. The words nearly stuck in my throat. I couldn't imagine getting a gold necklace with my name on it from a star like Raven Blaine. Randy had given me lots of things, though—valentines and Christmas cards, and an adorable stuffed white bear that I'd named Precious. My spirits slipped a notch when I remembered that I didn't even have Precious anymore. During the awful time when Randy had been in a coma after a hit-and-run accident, I'd been allowed to stay at the hospital;

before I left, I had given the bear to Lisa Pratt, the little girl who had been my roommate.

I sighed, but Taffy didn't seem to notice. "He sent me roses in a silver bowl, and invited me to a cast party, and asked me if I would date him if I come back to Hollywood," she went on excitedly.

"It sounds as though you had a terrific time," I mumbled. "It sure beats hanging around boring old Wakeman Junior High with a bunch of ordinary kids who aren't famous or anything. All we do is go to ball games and dances and movies at Cinema Six, and hang out at Bumpers, and eat lunch in the world's worst cafeteria. Nobody ever sees our school plays except our parents, and our school's television show is on local cable only. It's really the pits around here, compared with Hollywood. I'll bet you're dying to get back."

I couldn't believe I'd said all that. I even heard my voice getting louder as I went along. I was practically shouting by the end.

The silence that followed was deafening. Taffy was staring at me as if she'd just come face-to-face with a snake. I felt a little like a snake, too. I hadn't meant to say all that. It had just slipped out. Taffy Sinclair really was a big deal, whether I wanted to admit it or not. She had been places I'd never been and done things I'd never dreamed of doing. The truth was, I didn't know how to handle the new Taffy Sinclair.

Several seconds passed before Taffy said anything, and then she chose her words carefully. "Would you like to know a secret?" she asked in a small voice. The expression on her face was solemn, and her eyes were a little sad.

Reluctantly I nodded, thinking that anything she would want to confide in me about couldn't be very important.

Taffy took a deep breath and sat down on the bed beside me again. She was staring at the notebook and pen in my lap, and I quickly put them aside.

"To be perfectly honest," she began, "I really missed doing all those things you mentioned. They were the normal things I'd been doing all my life. Sometimes you don't realize how important something is until you have to give it up. And going to Hollywood was awfully scary at first. I'd never been so far away from home before, and all the other kids in the cast had been actors most of their lives. I was the ordinary kid to them, and I was terrified they'd make fun of my acting."

I couldn't believe she was saying this to me. "Did they?" I couldn't resist asking.

She nodded. "Well, only Paige did, but she was brutal. She kept calling me an amateur and trying to upstage me. But that was just until we got to know each other. Then I found out that she had thought she was getting the part I played and that she'd been furious when I got it."

"That must have been awful," I acknowledged.

It was hard to imagine Taffy Sinclair being the victim. I fought down the impulse to tell myself that she deserved it.

"Yeah," she said, nodding. "Paige and I were big rivals for everything at first. She even had a crush on Raven Blaine and couldn't stand it when he paid attention to me."

I looked at the floor the instant she said the word *rivals*. That's what Taffy and I had been, almost forever, and here she was talking about rivalry as if it were hardly anything to be concerned about. Of course she could feel that way. She was a movie star.

A series of pictures flashed in my mind like photographs being projected onto a screen. Taffy Sinclair blackmailing me when I tried to put Miss Wiggins's wallet back where I found it so no one would think I stole it. Taffy Sinclair trying to hog all the credit for helping me find baby Ashley. Taffy Sinclair matching up with *my boyfriend*, Randy Kirwan, when our class did a computer matchup. Taffy Sinclair trying to break up The Fab Five by luring Melanie into being a model with her. The pictures could have gone on forever, except that Taffy was talking again.

"There was actually one time when Paige convinced the director to change a whole scene around so that she would be in front of the camera instead of me," recalled Taffy with a little laugh.

"How can you laugh about a thing like that?" I asked in astonishment. "I'd be so angry."

I was sorry the instant the words were out. I didn't really want to reveal my inner feelings to Taffy Sinclair. There was no telling what she might do.

"Because when I got to know Paige better, I found out that it wasn't really me who was causing all her problems and keeping us from becoming friends. It was Paige herself."

"I don't get it," I told her.

Taffy gave me an understanding smile and continued, "She was down on herself. She felt inferior, and that made her hate me and feel jealous because I had the part she wanted. But the truth is, neither of us had understood how much we had in common. We both matured a lot when we realized that." She paused. She had the friendliest smile I had ever seen on her face, and she was looking straight at me.

I blinked as I realized what was happening. Taffy Sinclair was actually trying to make up with me!

I shot another quick look at the floor. Was this some kind of joke? Did she have a terrible trick up her sleeve? Did she have a movie camera and a tape recorder hidden somewhere in the room so that she could embarrass me in front of the whole world if I fell for it?

I let out a deep breath I didn't know I was holding. I had the strangest feeling that for once in her life, Taffy Sinclair was being sincere. As if on cue, something she had just said rang in my mind. *She was down on herself. She felt inferior, and that made her hate me and feel jealous . . .*

Hadn't I come over here feeling down on myself? Hadn't I felt inferior because she was a big-deal movie star and I was just plain Jana? Had she been able to read my mind?

Her words continued rolling through my mind. *But the truth is, neither one of us had understood how much we had in common. We both matured a lot when we realized that.*

Did Taffy Sinclair and I have a lot in common, too? Is that what she was trying to say? And then another word sprang out: *matured*. She had said that she and Paige matured a lot when they realized how much they had in common. Mr. Neal had used that word. He said he was sure we had both matured a lot since Mark Twain Elementary. Had we?

I glanced up at her again. Her face was calm. Her eyes were friendly. She didn't look as if she wanted to be anybody's rival.

I swallowed hard as the terrible truth hit home. Taffy Sinclair had grown up, and I hadn't. She had outmatured me by a mile. As hard as it was to believe, she wanted to be my friend.

The corners of my mouth began turning up, as if they had a mind of their own. I tried to keep from grinning like an idiot. Things were happening awfully fast. Did I really want to be Taffy Sinclair's friend?

Well, it would certainly beat being her enemy! argued a little voice in my head.

"So you and Paige became good friends?" I ventured in a whispery voice.

Taffy nodded. "Just as soon as we were able to tell each other we were sorry for the way we had acted."

Taking a deep breath, I plunged ahead before I could lose my nerve. "I guess it would be a good idea if you and I did that, too."

I felt prickly all over as I waited for her reply.

"That's what I thought," she replied a little shyly.

"We're much too *mature* to be enemies anymore," I declared with newfound confidence. "I guess I'd have to say that I'm really sorry that we were such babies before."

"Me, too," Taffy assured me. "It's such a waste of time to be enemies when we could have so much fun being friends."

"And we really do have a lot of things in common," I added. "Remember Miss Wiggins, our sixth-grade teacher, and how our class used to love to play jokes on her?"

"How could I forget," said Taffy, giggling. "Like the time we all sneezed at exactly the same instant."

"Right, and she went up and down the aisles handing out tissues and then made us all blow our noses."

I couldn't help laughing hard at the memory, but at the same time it seemed strange to be laughing along with Taffy Sinclair.

"And remember the computer matchup when *ten* girls matched up with Randy?" asked Taffy.

I nodded. "I was furious then," I admitted, "but now it just seems funny."

"That's because we're not enemies now," said Taffy.

I sighed. "Remember when we found baby Ashley? Remember how beautiful she was?"

"And how sweet," added Taffy. "She was the most wonderful baby in the world."

"Yeah, and we didn't want to tell anyone we had found her," I said. "We wanted to keep her for ourselves."

Neither one of us said anything for a moment. I guess we were both lost in our memories of baby Ashley. I know I was.

"We almost became friends then, didn't we?" asked Taffy.

"Almost," I admitted. "But since it didn't happen then, I'm glad it's happening now."

"Me, too," agreed Taffy, and I knew she meant it.

Suddenly I felt a little giddy, as if a big weight had been lifted off my shoulders. I had never realized before just how much hard work goes into hating someone.

I gave her a silly grin, and she gave me one back. Then I opened my notebook to my list of interview questions and said, "So tell me about all the famous people you met in Hollywood and the parties you went to and things like that. I'm dying to hear all about it."

And the funny thing about it was, I really wanted to know.

Unfortunately Taffy and I never got the time to enjoy our new friendship. The next week she was called back to Hollywood to start working on the television series based on her movie.

The feature page on Taffy turned out great, if I do say so myself, and I had promised to send her a copy of the yearbook. But I really wish she could be here at the dinner-dance to see it tonight, I thought. I know that even though she's in Hollywood, down deep she'd like to be here, too.

CHAPTER

2

Melanie Edwards looked around to see who had tapped her on the shoulder. It was Garrett Boldt, who was standing behind her chair and holding his copy of *The Wigwam*.

"Would you sign my yearbook?" he asked.

His smile was so big that Melanie wondered for an instant if Shane would get jealous. After all, she had dated Garrett a few times, and he was one of the best-looking boys in the eighth grade.

A quick glance told her that Shane was talking to Randy, so she gave Garrett a coy smile, and said, "I'd love to, but only if you'll sign mine."

"Sure," agreed Garrett, and the two exchanged books.

Melanie thought for a minute and then wrote: "To

25

Garrett Boldt, a good friend, and a great photographer who's one of the *flashiest* guys around. Ha, ha! Just kidding! Love, Melanie."

She handed his yearbook back and took hers, sneaking a peek at what he had written.

"Dear Melanie, You're as pretty as a picture and one of the sweetest girls at Wacko. See you in a year at high school. Garrett."

Melanie sighed as she closed the book. Maybe Garrett still liked her a little bit. She was so busy thinking over the possibility that she almost didn't hear Mr. Bell begin introducing each organization and talking about what it had accomplished during the year. To no one's surprise, the sports teams were called to the stage first, and the rest of the students gave them thunderous applause.

When the athletes had gone back to their seats, Mr. Bell went to the podium again. "It would have been just about impossible for our fine teams to have such a great season without the group of students I'm about to introduce—the *cheerleaders*!"

Melanie let out a whoop of joy as more applause rang out and Miss Wolfe, the cheerleading coach, hurried up to the stage.

"Oh, my gosh. What if I trip going up the stairs?" she whispered to Shane.

He gave her a confident look. "After all the acrobatics you did at the games? Don't worry. You won't trip."

Miss Wolfe leaned toward the microphone. "Ven

I call your name, please come up to da stage," she said in her thick German accent. "And audience, please hold your applause until everyone is up here."

Melanie straightened her dress and twirled a lock of her reddish-brown hair while she listened for her name.

"Dekeisha Adams, Beth Barry, Alexis Duvall, Melanie Edwards, Tammy Lucero, Laura McCall, Mandy McDermott, and our eighth member, who cannot be with us tonight, Taffy Sinclair," said Miss Wolfe.

Melanie rose to her feet and marched proudly to the stage along with Beth. She didn't dare look at any of the other members of the squad for fear she'd burst out giggling.

She was so excited that she barely heard Miss Wolfe talk about the great year they had had. When the applause finally died down and the seven girls left the stage, Melanie went back to her seat thinking about how much fun she had had on the seventh-grade cheerleading squad. Tryouts had been scary, and some of the girls, such as Jana, hadn't made it. Melanie still couldn't believe she had been one of the lucky ones. She had loved cheering at the games and meeting the cheerleaders from other schools.

Melanie looked again at the picture of the seventh-grade cheerleading squad on page 214 in the yearbook and giggled as another memory suddenly popped into her mind. Cheerleading clinic at Old Trinity College. Now that had been a weekend to remember. . . .

MELANIE'S MEMORY

After school on that cold, dreary Friday afternoon with snow clouds threatening overhead, Mom loaded the entire seventh-grade cheerleading squad and our luggage into the Teen Taxi van. Laura and Tammy got in first, jumped into one corner of the back bench, and immediately began whispering together. Alexis and Dekeisha squeezed onto the bench seat beside them. Beth, Mandy, and I took the seats behind the driver. Taffy Sinclair was the only member of the squad missing. She was in Hollywood making a movie. Finally Miss Wolfe climbed into the passenger seat next to Mom for the hour-and-a-half drive to Old Trinity.

At least the drive usually took an hour and a half, I remembered sadly, but this time it took three hours because halfway there the van had a flat tire. To make matters worse, as soon as the flat was fixed, snow began to fall, reducing traffic to a crawl.

By the time we finally arrived at Old Trinity, all the other squads had already checked in, gotten their dormitory room assignments, and begun getting acquainted.

"At least you and I are rooming together," said Beth, when the preppy-looking college girl at the front desk handed both of us packets containing a key for room 113, meal tickets for the cafeteria, and information about the dorm.

"Hey, it says that our suitemates are from Nathan Hale Junior High in Danbury," I read aloud as we lugged our suitcases down the corridor where adjoining rooms 113 and 114, which made up our suite, were located. I was feeling pretty upbeat until I read a little farther. "And—oh, my gosh!—their names are Bob B. Shapkoff and George Holiman!"

We stopped in our tracks and blinked at each other in horror. *"Boys!"* we cried in unison.

I gulped hard. "Lots of schools have boys on their squads," I said in a shaky voice. My insides were shaking, too, as I visualized some of the muscle-bound hunks I'd seen leading cheers for other schools sleeping in the beds next door to us and taking showers in *our* bathroom.

"Don't panic," said Beth, even though her voice was trembling. "We'll go back to the lobby and talk to the girl who checked us in. This has to be a mistake."

"Right," I said. "They would never have us rooming with *boys*!"

We raced back to the check-in desk, but no one was there, and the lobby was deserted.

"Oh, no!" I groaned. "Where did she go?"

Beth shrugged. "I guess she left. You and I were

the last two members of the last squad to check in, remember?"

"Well, we've got to talk to somebody," I insisted, looking around helplessly. "And we don't have any idea where Mom and Miss Wolfe are. I think the chaperons are staying on a different floor."

"Why don't we dump our stuff in our room and then find somebody to talk to," suggested Beth.

I stared at her in disbelief. "But what if *they* are there? You know I like boys, but not for *roommates*!"

"Mel, calm down," ordered Beth. "They're our *suite*mates, not our *room*mates. And the literature about the clinic said there would be a bathroom between the two rooms in each suite."

"Yeah, but we share the bathroom," I reminded her. "I'll die if we have to share a bathroom with two boys, no matter how cute they are." Then a horrible thought occurred to me. "What if one of *them* walks in when *one of us* is in there?"

Beth didn't say anything for a moment, and I knew she was thinking over that possibility.

Finally she sighed and said, "Come on. Let's dump all this stuff and go look for someone to talk to—*fast*."

I fell in step with her, and we hurried along the ground-floor hallway, checking the numbers on the doors. "It sure is quiet," I said. "I wonder where everybody is?"

Beth shifted her suitcase so that she could look at

her watch. "Eeek! It's almost time for dinner. Most kids have probably already gone to the cafeteria."

I looked around the dimly lit hall and felt uneasy. What if Bob and George weren't the only boys staying in these rooms? What if we had accidentally been assigned to a room on an all-boy floor!

"Come on," I urged. "Let's hurry."

Beth set down her suitcase, put her lavender makeup case on the floor beside it, and unlocked the door to room 113. Then she pushed the door open a crack and peeked inside.

I tried to look over her shoulder, but the room was dark. "What do you see? Are they in there?"

"They wouldn't be in our room," Beth replied, but I could see that she was holding her breath as she pushed the door open. "See? What did I tell you?" she said triumphantly. "Nobody here. We've got the place to ourselves."

Beth lifted her suitcase onto the bed by the window, and I put mine on the bed next to hers, still looking around for signs of boys.

"I don't think we should unpack," I told her. "They'll probably move us to another room, anyway."

"Right," agreed Beth. She started back toward the hall and stopped, eyeing a narrow door on one side of the room. "That must be the bathroom," she murmured.

I looked nervously at the bathroom door, feeling goosebumps rising on my arms. What if Bob and George were in there . . . listening to our conversation . . . making plans to spy . . . I gulped and made a beeline for the door leading to the hall.

"Wait," called Beth. "Let's at least look in the bathroom."

"What for?" I demanded. Had she lost her mind? I wanted to get out of there, and fast.

"You know, guys' stuff," answered Beth. "Like shaving gear and things."

"Beth Barry," I said, rolling my eyes, "you know as well as I do that seventh-grade boys don't shave."

"Okay, okay, but guys' stuff is different than girls' stuff. You can bet there won't be any lipstick or blusher."

Maybe she had a point, I thought. We could find out if Bob and George had checked in to our suite, and now was the best time to find out, since we were both dressed. I took a deep breath and tiptoed to the bathroom door, tapping softly. "Anyone in there?"

No answer.

"Go ahead," urged Beth. "Open it."

I looked back at Beth for reassurance and then reached for the knob, but the moment I touched it I drew my hand back in panic. "You do it," I begged. "I don't have the nerve."

"Oh, all right." Beth waved me aside and muttered out of the corner of her mouth, "You're just a big chicken, Melanie Edwards."

Beth yanked the door open and stared in. Motioning with a nod of her head, she said, "Nothing. No boys' stuff. No girls' stuff. It's totally empty."

"Maybe they aren't here yet," I said.

"Naw. Remember the girl at the front desk said we were the last ones to check in. If everybody else is already here, that means Bob and George aren't our suitemates after all." Beth began bouncing excitedly. "We have the whole suite to ourselves."

"Yeah," I said eagerly. "And they probably just forgot to take their name off the room assignment list."

"Terrific!" yelled Beth. She skipped across the narrow bathroom and grabbed the door on the other side, leading to the room Bob and George would have shared. But just as she jerked it open, I saw something move in the second bedroom.

"Surprise! Surprise!" yelled two girls, jumping out in front of us. They doubled over with laughter.

"We thought you'd never get here!" exclaimed one of them, a short, sandy-haired girl with freckles.

I gulped in big breaths and tried to speak. "Who . . . I mean, what . . ."

"Yeah, who are you?" murmured Beth from beside her.

"I'm Bob B.—you know, Bobbi," said the other girl, who wore her shiny black hair in a long French braid. "And this is George. She likes to be called George instead of Georgia."

"Right," said George. "That was a pretty good joke, wasn't it? We knew you'd think your suite-mates were boys, and we were dying for you to get here so we could see your faces." The two girls winked at each other and laughed again.

Beth and I wobbled against each other in relief and began laughing, too. These two girls were totally off the wall, but they were going to be lots of fun. Nodding at George, I murmured, "Yeah, that was a pretty good joke."

After Beth and I introduced ourselves, Beth still looked puzzled. "But how did you get them to let you sign up as Bob B. and George?"

"Simple," replied Bobbi. "We just said those were our nicknames. I mean, so what if you thought we were boys for a few minutes? We aren't, so what's the harm?"

"And George really is what I go by," the sandy-haired girl assured us. "Imagine naming your kid after the state you were born in, which is exactly what my parents did. The only state I like well enough to want to be named after is Hawaii. That's why I started going by George."

"Hawaii Holiman," mused Beth. "Hey, I like it! It sounds like show biz."

"In case you haven't noticed, George is a big practical joker," said Bobbi. "It was her idea to make you think we were boys."

"Don't let her kid you," George told us. "She always loves to be in on my gags."

Bobbi giggled and then glanced at her watch. "Oh, my gosh! If we don't get to the cafeteria immediately, we're going to miss dinner."

"And we definitely don't want to do that, since we've got a big joke cooked up," added George. A sly grin spread over her freckled face, and she called back over her shoulder as she and Bobbi headed into the hall, "We'll tell you your part in it on the way to the cafeteria."

Beth and I exchanged wide-eyed glances as we followed. *What are we getting ourselves into?* I wondered as a tingle traveled up my spine.

The building that housed the cafeteria was next door to the dorm, so the four of us didn't bother to put our coats on for the short dash through the snow.

When we clustered inside the front door to stamp slush off our tennis shoes, George draped arms over Beth's and my shoulders and said confidentially, "Don't forget what you're supposed to do."

"I don't know," I said. "Are you sure we ought to be doing this? What if we get in trouble?"

"Melanie, you're such a chicken," complained Beth. It was obvious that Beth was totally awed by George. *But what would happen if we got caught?*

"I am not a chicken," I insisted. "Don't forget, my mom's one of the chaperons. She'll have a fit if she thinks I'm not behaving myself."

"Come on, Mel, your mother was a kid once." Turning to George, Beth added, "She'll do it. I'll make sure."

I rolled my eyes and followed the others toward the cafeteria. At least if I got in trouble, I wouldn't have to face the consequences alone.

The college student checking meal tickets at the door was a skinny boy with a beak nose. He was reading a thick book, probably a textbook, and waved us through with barely a glance at our tickets.

"Okay," George whispered as we got in the line, "this is it. Everybody remember what you're supposed to do, and *above all* keep your cool."

Bobbi was first, followed by George, then me, and Beth brought up the rear. My heart thudded like crazy as I watched George unzip her shoulder bag and rest her hand on something inside.

I can't believe I'm doing this, I thought.

The cafeteria was filling up with seventh-grade cheerleaders from several nearby towns. There were a lot of cute boys scattered at tables around the room, and I chuckled, remembering how panicked Beth and I had been just a few moments ago, thinking that we might be sharing a suite with two of them.

I glanced at Bobbi and George as I took a tray and selected a bacon cheeseburger from the steam table, thinking we couldn't have been luckier. I was a little scared about what we were going to do, but I was excited, too. I could tell that our suitemates were the most fun of any kids at the clinic.

George nudged me. "Go on," she urged. "Start talking to the kids in line behind you. We're almost there."

Beth was already in conversation with a couple of girls who were behind us in line. At least a dozen more boys and girls were coming into the cafeteria.

"Hi," I said to one of the girls. "I'm Melanie Edwards from Wakeman." I plastered a fake grin on my face, afraid to look at Beth because we might burst out laughing.

"Hi, I'm Staci Berkowitz," replied one of them, who had reddish-blond hair.

"And I'm Morgan Miller," volunteered the blond beside her.

"Is this the first time you've ever been to a cheerleading clinic?" I asked.

I tried to keep the conversation flowing and keep an eye on Bobbi and George at the same time. Bobbi was the lookout, watching the kitchen workers behind the steam tables for the right moment, when none of them was looking in her or George's direction. When the moment was right, Bobbi gave George a quick signal, and George opened her purse and pulled out an incredibly real-looking fake brownie on a small paper plate. Next she pulled out a bright red cherry and plopped it on top of the brownie. With unbelievable speed, George reached into the dessert section and set the fake brownie among the real ones. Then she casually took a piece of apple pie for herself and slid her tray forward toward the beverages.

I almost passed out on the spot. George was absolutely amazing! I wanted to laugh out loud, but I didn't dare.

Bobbi made a beeline for an empty table. "Hurry," she said breathlessly. "Let's watch to see who gets it."

George was grinning from ear to ear. "I put the cherry on it so that we could be sure which one it was, and I put it toward the back so that we could get to our table in time to watch who takes it."

"George, you're a genius," Beth squealed. "This is going to be a scream."

I was nodding. "We're going to have to remember all this stuff and try it ourselves when we get back to Wakeman."

"Uh-oh," said Bobbi. "Look who's coming in now. The faculty advisors and the chaperons."

I glanced toward the line and almost exploded. "But one of the chaperons is my mother," I wailed. "She's third in line."

"Don't sweat it," said George. "So what if one of them gets the fake brownie. Nobody knows who put it there." She nonchalantly dragged a French fry through a blob of ketchup and popped it into her mouth.

I closed my eyes. I couldn't bear to watch. "Beth, you watch and tell me who gets the brownie. Oh, please! Don't let it be my mom!"

Beth patted my arm reassuringly. "She's getting her tray now. Now she's getting her silverware and a napkin," reported Beth in a monotone voice. "She's getting a plate of something—spaghetti, I think— and now she's looking at the salads. Nope. No salad. She's moving toward the desserts."

I grabbed Beth's hand. "Now what?"

Nobody at the table said anything for a moment. Finally Beth said in a small voice, "Mel . . . I hate to tell you this . . ."

"She got it?" My eyes flew open in astonishment.

"No," whispered Beth. "It's worse. Miss Wolfe got it."

"One of your chaperons?" asked Bobbi.

I nodded miserably. "Our faculty advisor. She is really tough on kids who break the rules. Do you think we could get kicked off the squad if she finds out we were in on this?"

George leaned across the table, looking first me and then Beth straight in the eye. "Keep your cool, remember? Like I said, nobody knows who put it there. That's the fun of jokes like this." A mischievous grin spread across her face again.

"Right," Bobbi chimed in. "So it's a fake brownie. It isn't as if it were poison or something. What's the harm?"

"I hope you're right," I murmured. "I *really* hope you're right."

I couldn't swallow another bite as I watched Miss

Wolfe sit down at a table near the back of the cafeteria and begin eating.

"What's she doing?" asked Beth. "I can't see her
from where I'm sitting."

"She's buttering a roll," I said. "Maybe she'll get
too full to eat her dessert." I looked around hope-
fully.

"I think Beth was right. You're a chicken," remarked George.

I gave George a dirty look and glanced at Miss
Wolfe again. She was sitting at the table with Mom,
and the two of them were talking and smiling as if
nothing in the world could possibly be wrong. Just
wait! I thought miserably.

"Now what's she doing?" asked Beth.

"Taking a sip of coffee. Oh, no! She's pushing
her plate aside and reaching for her dessert!"

Beth plastered herself against me, craning her
neck to see Miss Wolfe. "Yeah, it's the brownie! I
can see the cherry on top."

"Quick! Turn around and don't look!" ordered
George.

Slowly Beth and I faced the center of the table.
I tried not to freak out, but it was pretty hard to
stay calm. Was this joke really going to be funny,
anyway?

I didn't have long to wait for the answer. An
instant later a loud *SQUAWK*! came from the direction of Miss Wolfe's table.

"Now you can look!" George said, laughing.

I whipped around. Miss Wolfe was standing beside her table looking startled, and that wasn't all. Kids at the tables around her were breaking up with laughter. Gradually Miss Wolfe's expression changed from surprise to amusement, and she poked gingerly at the brownie with her fork.

SQUAWK! The plastic brownie sounded exactly like an enormous dog toy. *SQUAWK! SQUAWK!* it went again as Miss Wolfe kept poking it with her fork.

Finally she held up her hand for quiet. I couldn't believe that she was smiling. "Okay, everybody. The joke is over. It vas a super joke, and whoever dreamed it up is a great comedian. Now ve vill please go back to eating."

As the gym teacher sat down again, I shook my head in amazement. "She wasn't mad. I can't believe that she was such a good sport about the whole thing."

"See?" Bobbi and George said in unison. Then George added, "Why would she get mad? It was just a fake brownie. What's the harm?"

George was right, and the whole idea was making me hyper. I had never imagined that playing jokes could be so much fun. How could I have been so lucky to meet Bobbi and George?

That night we sat up talking in Bobbi and George's room until one of the chaperons knocked on the door at ten o'clock and announced that it was time for lights out. Later, snuggled in bed, I had a hard time going to sleep. I was still awake when the chaperon came back again half an hour later for bed check. I couldn't stop thinking about George. She had said that she thought up most of her own jokes and read about others in magazines and joke books. She also said that she bought things in a shop that specialized in magic tricks and gags, like the fake brownie that squawked like a dog toy. I finally drifted off, thinking that I couldn't remember ever having so much fun.

Brrrrrrrrrrr!

"I can't believe it's morning already," I grumbled, shutting off the alarm clock on the bedside table. Beth was already up and dressed in her cheerleading uniform.

"Come on, sleepy head," she chirped. "This is the day we've been waiting for."

I yawned and pulled myself out of bed. By the time I had brushed my teeth and put on my short, red pleated skirt and gold sweater with matching red lettering, my energy was surging. Today was going to be a big day.

"I could hear Bobbi and George talking when I was in the bathroom," said Beth. "We'll have to see them later, though. Miss Wolfe wants our squad to eat breakfast and then meet her beside the trophy case in the lobby of the gym at seven-thirty sharp."

"Eeek! It's five after seven already," I cried, grabbing my jacket and heading for the door.

The slush on the sidewalk had frozen over night, and we slipped and slid to the gymnasium after gulping down a fast breakfast. At seven-thirty sharp we stood by the trophy case with Miss Wolfe and the five other Wakeman cheerleaders, waiting to go into the gym. The lobby was mobbed with cheerleaders in bright uniforms. Next to us a squad in green and white was bouncing on their toes and snapping fingers as they chanted the words to a yell. Excitement was everywhere. Kids chattered happily, waving to each other, and racing to greet friends from other squads.

While we waited, Miss Wolfe handed out the schedule for the day. "Our first class vill be tumbling," she announced over the noisy crowd. "Ve vill be in class vith four other squads."

We read over our schedules and murmured excitedly among ourselves. Finally Miss Wolfe signaled for us to enter the gym. "Ve vill all stay together," she commanded.

I was disappointed that the groups in the tumbling class did not include Bobbi and George's squad from Nathan Hale.

"Have you seen our suitemates anywhere?" I whispered to Beth later during a break.

"Nope," said Beth. "We'll look for them at lunch."

The morning went by unbelievably fast. The

tumbling routines we learned weren't as hard as I'd expected, and in the next class the new pyramid routines were terrific.

"I didn't think lunchtime would ever get here," said Dekeisha when we headed for the cafeteria. "I'm *starved*!"

My stomach rumbled in agreement.

"Watch for Bobbi and George," said Beth.

"I think I see them!" I cried, pointing to a girl with a long, black French braid and a small, sandy-haired companion standing near the door. They were searching the faces in the crowd. "It is them, and they're looking for us."

"Hey, you two, wait till you hear what we've got cooked up for this afternoon," George began as soon as we walked up.

"You're not going to pull a joke during the clinic, are you?" I asked in horror.

George's freckled face was beaming. "Of course!"

"I don't know," I replied slowly. I frowned and nodded toward the stands where most of the chaperons were seated in small groups. "My mom's up there watching us. I know she'd see me if I tried to pull something crazy."

"Not to worry," sang Bobbi. "We've already taken care of this one. You guys don't have to do a thing."

"Right," confirmed George. Her eyes were twinkling. "Just sit back and watch the masters at work."

"What are you going to do?" asked Beth.

"And when?" I said. "How will we know it's time?"

George threw back her head and laughed. "You'll know."

"I'm famished." Bobbi suddenly changed the subject. "Come on. Let's get in line."

I devoured three tacos while the four of us compared schedules. "I can't believe that we don't have a class with you guys until the last one of the day," I complained.

"Hey, but that's the best one," said George. "That's when we work on jumps, including the Herkie, which is only the most famous cheerleading jump in history."

"And the hardest," added Bobbi.

"Yipes! It's time to go already," said Beth, jumping up and heading for the tray return.

I scrambled to follow her. "We're off to the modern dance room. We're supposed to work on definition of movement in front of the practice mirrors. See you later."

Beth and I went through our afternoon classes, keeping an eye open and an ear cocked for some sign of George's latest practical joke. In the gymnasium large groups of multiple squads formed classes to work on different phases of cheerleading. There were flashes of color as cheerleaders sprang into the air, and the noise was almost deafening. But it was fun, and by the time the announcement came over the loudspeaker that the last class of the afternoon was ready to begin, I had forgotten all of my nervousness over the joke George and Bobbi had promised to pull.

"Okay, kids! The class on jumps is over here!" The handsome, athletic-looking instructor, wearing an Old Trinity cheerleading sweater, was motioning us toward one corner of the gym floor near the stage. "It's time to get the lead out!"

For the next half hour we worked at perfecting the Flying Dutchman, the Spread Eagle, and of course the famous Herkie.

"Chins up! Keep your backs straight!" the instructor shouted over and over again.

I tried hard. There was so much to remember. Keep perfect posture. Don't let your arms get flappy. Point your toes. Keep your fingers together. If any kids think being a cheerleader is easy, they're crazy!

I was just about to drop from exhaustion when the public address system suddenly crackled to life. All around the huge gym boys and girls suddenly stopped talking, staring at the speakers hanging in the rafters high above them.

I looked around and frowned. What was going on? Suddenly I knew. I shot a quick look at George. She nodded at me, battling to hold down the corners of her mouth and keep from smiling. I gulped. This was it!

Suddenly band music blared out of the loudspeakers, and a cheer went up from Bobbi and George's squad.

"It's our fight song!" shouted a tall, dark-haired cheerleader standing next to Bobbi.

"Come on!" shouted George. "Let's show them *Nathan Hale spirit*!"

While the rest of us looked on in dumbfounded silence, George led her squad onto the stage, where they got in formation and began singing the words to the song.

> "We're loyal to you, Nathan Hale!
> We're orange and blue, Nathan Hale!"

"Can you believe this?" shouted Beth. She was gesturing around the huge gym, where kids were beginning to hum along with Nathan Hale's fight song. "Talk about nerve!"

"Yeah," I admitted, clapping my hands to the rhythm. "You really have to hand it to George."

The fight song went on for a full five minutes, with George and her squad leading the entire gym in song. When it was finally over, the room rocked with thunderous applause.

I turned to Beth. "Nobody is going to forget Nathan Hale Junior High *or* its cheerleaders for a long, long time."

* * *

Everyone was still talking about the Nathan Hale fight song at dinner that night, and George and Bobbi were the heroes of the day. Even Laura McCall and Tammy Lucero seemed impressed.

"How did you have the nerve to pull that off?" Tammy asked George.

"And you didn't even get in trouble," added Dekeisha. "If that had been me . . ." Her voice trailed off sadly.

If that had been me, too! I thought as I remembered my mom sitting in the bleachers all day long, watching everything that went on. I'd be dead by now, or at least grounded for the rest of my life.

George and Bobbi entertained the girls at the table with stories of other jokes they'd pulled. There was the time they put stinky cheese on the ancient radiators in the math classroom. They had done it on a cold winter day when their teacher was giving a killer test, and halfway through the exam the room had to be evacuated because of the smell.

"We had to keep a low profile on that one," Bobbi admitted over the giggles of the others. "We could have really gotten into trouble."

"But most of your jokes are pretty innocent, right?" I said. "They're just funny and don't hurt anybody."

"Exactly," assured George.

"I just wish my mom weren't here," I said, sighing.

When we finished eating, the four of us headed

back for the dorm. A crowd had gathered in the lounge to watch television, and other kids were standing around in the halls talking.

"I don't know about you guys, but I'm beat," said Beth. "They really worked us today."

"Me, too," I murmured.

"Why don't you come to our room again," offered Bobbi. "We had a lot of fun last night just sitting around and talking. And don't forget, tomorrow we go home."

"Sounds good to me," I replied.

"Me, too," Beth and George agreed in unison.

"We're really going to miss you guys," I said when we were all settled in Bobbi and George's room a few minutes later. "This weekend has been a ball."

"Yeah." George sounded wistful. "Not everybody enjoys practical jokes as much as you two do."

We talked for a long time, telling each other about school, boyfriends, and all the things we liked to do best. Beth explained about the plays she had been in and the television show Wakeman produced on the local cable channel. I tried not to talk about boys too much, and I even admitted that my mother had embarrassed the living daylights out of me when she started the Teen Taxi.

Suddenly Bobbi announced, "I don't know about you guys, but all this conversation has made me hungry. And guess what? I saw a pizza place just a couple of blocks away."

George's eyes brightened. "Are you thinking what I'm thinking?"

George and Bobbi began giggling.

"You're not thinking of sneaking out, are you?" I asked apprehensively. "You know we're not supposed to leave the building."

"What's wrong with sneaking out?" asked Beth. "We're on the ground floor. All we have to do is unlock the window, slip out and get the pizza, and then slip back in again. It's only eight-thirty; it's an hour and a half until lights out. Nobody will ever know we're gone."

"That's the spirit," said George.

"But what if something goes wrong?" I insisted.

The other three girls looked at each other, nodded, and chorused, "Melanie's a chicken."

"I've got an idea," piped up Bobbi. "Melanie, you can stay here and be our lookout. That way you can get rid of anyone who comes looking for us."

"Right," said George. "You can watch for us and open the window when you see us coming."

"Would you do it, Mel?" begged Beth.

I bit my lip. "Well . . ."

"You'll be totally safe," Beth argued. "There's no way you can get into any trouble."

I sighed and thought about Mom and Miss Wolfe, somewhere in this very building. Still, just as Beth said, if I stayed right here, I couldn't possibly get into trouble. And pizza did sound terrific.

"Okay," I agreed before I could lose my nerve, "I'll do it. But be careful. And hurry!"

The others bundled up in jackets, mittens, and scarves and headed for the window in our room.

George tried to twist the heavy lock, but it wouldn't budge. "Wow! I'll bet this window hasn't been opened in ages. The lock's all rusted. I think it's stuck forever."

"Let me try it," offered Beth after George and Bobbi had both tugged unsuccessfully on the lock.

Beth worked at it while the others looked on. "I think it's coming," she whispered. With a grunt of determination, Beth made one last attempt to twist the lock. This time it turned. "Hey, I did it!" she shouted.

Beth and George carefully raised the window, and the three of them slid out onto the snow-covered ground.

"Don't forget, *hurry*!" I called after them.

A moment later they were out of sight. I lowered the window, closed the drapes, and sat down on the edge of my bed to wait. It was 8:41. How long would it take to race to the pizza place, put in an order, wait for it to be ready, and then hurry back? I thought about how much fun Beth was having sneaking around with George and Bobbi. Beth loved anything dramatic, and they were probably giggling their heads off and throwing snowballs at each other.

Suddenly I felt a sharp stab of loneliness. I was totally left out, *and it was my own fault.*

I stood up and shot an angry look at the window. Why am I such a chicken? Why didn't I go with them? Nothing was going to happen. They would sneak back in this window, and nobody would ever know the difference. And then *they* would have a big story to tell everybody when they got home.

I sank back onto the bed. And what would I have to tell everybody? That I sat by the window and waited.

I looked at my watch again. Had it been only five minutes since the others left? I stood up and paced the floor for a while, hating every minute that I was missing out on the fun.

Suddenly there was a knock at the door. "Who— who—" My voice seemed stuck in my throat. I cleared it and tried again. "Who is it?"

"It's Dekeisha. What are you guys doing in your rooms? Everybody else is in the lounge dancing and having a blast—*including the boys from the third floor!*"

I almost exploded. Boys from the third floor! Rats! *Everybody* was having fun except me. I looked around helplessly. I couldn't tell Dekeisha what was really going on, even though Dekeisha was a good friend. I had promised the others to cover for them, and besides, Dekeisha might accidentally slip in front of one of the chaperons and give everything away.

"Okay, Dekeisha," I called back. "We'll be down

in a little while. We're...uh...we're getting cleaned up. Okay?"

"Okay," Dekeisha replied.

I listened to her footsteps die away. I had to do something. I couldn't be the only person at the whole cheerleading clinic sitting in her room doing absolutely nothing. I sat down on my bed and stared at the window again. Surely the others would be back soon. Then we could all go down to the lounge and dance. And probably George would think of another practical joke to play.

A practical joke? I cocked an eyebrow at myself in the mirror. Why couldn't I play a joke on George, Bobbi, and Beth? It would be fun, and it would serve them right.

I sprang into action, locking the window and closing the drapes. "I'll pretend I've left the room," I whispered gleefully. "And everybody is in the lounge, so if they knock on other windows, nobody will hear them. And with the drapes closed, they won't be able to look in and see me breaking up the whole time."

Of course I won't let them stand out there so long that the pizza gets cold, I told myself as I returned to my bed. Plumping up the pillow, I leaned back to wait.

"That really was a workout today," I murmured. "I'm exhausted—and starved."

The next sound I heard was footsteps in the hall and the murmur of voices. I sat up with a start and looked at my watch. It was a quarter to ten. "Oh, my gosh!" I gasped. "I must have fallen asleep!" It was only fifteen minutes until lights out.

Where were Beth and Bobbi and George?

It took a couple of minutes to force the lock to turn. Sticking my head out the window, I looked around frantically. The snow-covered landscape was silent and empty. Maybe they were hiding behind a bush or something. "Beth? George? Bobbi?" I called softly.

No answer.

Raising my voice slightly, I tried again. "Beth! George! Bobbi!"

Still no answer.

There were lots of footprints in the snow. In fact, a well trodden path ran from the window to the sidewalk, which meant the girls had come back to the window several times and hadn't been able to get in.

My face flamed with guilt, and I began to panic. *Where were they?* Footprints dimpled the snow all up and down the side of the building. My mind began to spin as I imagined what had happened. My friends had returned to the window, only to find it locked. When they knocked and couldn't rouse me, they tried tapping on other windows, but all the cheerleaders were in the lounge dancing. At least they were until a few minutes ago, when the sound of girls returning to their rooms for the night had awakened me. But where were Beth, George, and Bobbi now?

"I only meant to play a joke," I sobbed. "Oh, why did I have to go to sleep?"

I considered the situation a moment and then slipped over the windowsill and into the crisp night air. Most of the buildings were dark, but across the quadrangle bright lights glowed in the windows of another dormitory. A few students hurried back and forth across the campus, but none of them was Beth or Bobbi or George.

I took a deep breath and called their names again, not really expecting an answer. Suddenly the light from the pizza restaurant a block or so away caught my eye. Had they returned there when they couldn't get into the dorm? It was a definite possibility. The pizza place was warm and well lighted. They would be safe there, while they tried to figure out what to do. Oh, please, I prayed, let them be there.

"Maybe I should go after them," I whispered, but I knew instantly that I couldn't do that. I had to stay where I was, because it was almost time for the chaperon to come around telling us it was lights out. And in another few minutes it would be time for bed check. I had to be there to cover for them at lights out, and *they* would have to be back by bed check!

I scrambled back into my room, shut the window, and hurried to the door, listening for sounds in the hall. It was quiet now, and I could imagine all of the kids safe in their rooms, getting ready for bed.

All except Beth, Bobbi, and George. I raced back to the window. The lights of the pizza place blazed in red and green. Were they there? Or were they somewhere out in the snow?

I know! I thought. I'll call the pizza place! Rummaging through my jeans pockets, I found a quarter. I remembered seeing a pay phone in the lobby. *If* I could get to it without being stopped by a nosy chaperon, and *if* there was a phone book nearby, and *if* I could figure out which pizza place it was among all the ones listed, since I couldn't read the sign from my room, then *maybe* I could find my friends.

Opening the door a crack, I peered outside. All was quiet in the hall. I could hear laughter coming from some of the rooms, but when I stuck my head out and looked around, no one was in sight.

"So far, so good," I whispered. I slipped into the hall, trying to be as silent as a shadow, and half tiptoed, half ran to the door leading to the lobby. I looked through the glass pane at the top of the door. My luck was holding. The lobby was empty, too. And directly across from the door was the pay phone *and a telephone book*.

Holding my breath, I ran to the phone and grabbed the book, turning to the yellow pages and thumbing frantically toward the section marked PIZZA. But an instant later I sucked in my breath. "There must be fifty listings! Oh, no. Which one is it?" I cried. "I only have one quarter."

I had no idea of the name or the address. I closed my eyes, trying to remember if I had seen the sign with the restaurant's name on it when I was standing outside in the snow. I was sure I hadn't, but I squeezed my eyes shut anyway, trying desperately to conjure up a picture of a sign.

"It's no use," I muttered. I was near tears as I ran a finger down the listings, looking for something—*anything*—that sounded familiar. Antipasto & Pizza? Caruso's Pizza? Dino's Pizza? Giuseppe's Pizza?. Luigi's Pizzeria? Nunzio's Pizza & Subs? Oh, I don't have any idea!

Putting down the phone book, I started to leave when I noticed some signs tacked to the wall around the phone. There were hand-lettered notices advertising students who tutored Russian and trigonometry, but there were also flyers about things like student trips to Europe and—my mouth dropped open when I saw it—That's Amoré Pizza! "Eat in or carry out. Fast delivery. *Just one block from campus*," the sign said, and it gave the phone number.

My hands were shaking as I dropped my one and only quarter in the slot and punched in the numbers. Oh please, let them be there! I prayed silently as I listened to the ringing of the phone.

"That's Amoré Pizza. Can I take your order?" The man's voice was pleasant, but my heart beat faster, anyway.

"Um, is this the place . . . I mean, are there three girls . . ." I fumbled.

"Hey, are you looking for some cheerleaders? They're right here. Just a minute." He was gone only an instant and then was back. "You're not a chaperon, are you?"

"No! Please put one of them on. This is important!"

"Just kidding," said the man. "Hold on a sec."

Thankfully the next voice I heard was Beth's. "Mel! What happened? Where were you? We pounded and pounded on the window, but you weren't there!"

I grimaced. "It's a long story. I'll explain everything later. You've just got to get back here NOW!"

"Okay," said Beth. "But you'd better be at that window this time, or we're dead."

"Don't worry," I assured her. "I'll be there."

I hung up the phone and glanced at my watch. Eeek! It was two minutes after ten already. The chaperons might be making rounds this very minute! I dashed to the corridor where my room was located, stopping short when I saw a chaperon at the far end of the hall knocking on the door to one of the rooms. I blinked when I realized who the chaperon was. My own mother.

"Now what am I going to do?" I whispered in a panicky voice. "What'll I say if she sees me?"

I flattened myself against the wall, moving slowly and trying to stay in the shadows. Mom was on the other side of the hallway, but she was moving in my direction. Every time Mom stopped to knock on a door, I dashed a little farther, coming to an abrupt stop whenever she showed signs of looking my way. My pulse throbbed in my temples. What else can go wrong? I wanted to shout.

Finally I reached my door. I waited until my mother's head was turned and jumped into the room, closing the door behind myself and leaning against it, panting hard.

Just let me get through this, and I'll never play another practical joke as long as I live, I prayed silently. A moment later a sharp rap sounded on the door.

I threw myself on my bed and tried to sound casual as I called, "Yes? Who is it?"

"It's me, honey," my mom answered. "Mind if I come in for a minute? We've hardly seen each other all day."

I buried my face in my pillow to muffle the groan escaping my lips. If this is a nightmare, please let me wake up!

I raced back to the door and opened it a crack. "Gosh, Mom, I'd let you in, but Beth's asleep and so are our suitemates. Besides, don't you have to do bed check in a few minutes?"

Mom shook her head. "Miss Wolfe is doing that tonight."

I froze at the thought that Miss Wolfe, of all people, might catch my three friends sneaking in through the window, and I almost didn't hear Mom saying, "I know you're tired, sweetheart. Sleep tight. I'll see you in the morning."

I hurried to the window, threw open the drapes, and looked outside. There was no sign of my three friends yet. Surely they would be here any moment.

"I know," I whispered to myself. "I'll go ahead and unlock the window. That way they'll be able to get in this time *no matter what*."

Next I went to the door and opened it just enough to see that Miss Wolfe had already started her rounds. Closing it, I bounced up and down nervously. What should I do? Miss Wolfe would be here any minute.

Back to the window. No one in sight. Over to Beth's bed. Make it look like she's there.

Frantically I pulled the clothes out of Beth's suitcase and stuffed them under the covers, plumping the bulge to make it look as if a person were lying there.

Back to the window. No one there yet! Where were they? Into Bobbi and George's room. Panting like crazy. Stuff clothes in their beds. Back to the window.

"Oh, my gosh!" I cried softly. "Here they come!"

Across the campus I could see the three girls bounding through the snow, heading straight for the dorm. I blinked hard to be sure I wasn't seeing things. George was carrying a pizza!

The sound of my own laughter was drowned out by a knock at the door. I leapt to attention. Miss Wolfe! She was here for bed check, and Beth and Bobbi and George would get to the window any second.

There was only one thing to do. I flipped the light switch off. Then I gave the lock on the window a sharp twist and pulled the drapes together. The girls would have to stay out there until I got rid of Miss Wolfe!

"Coming," I called. I ran to the door and started to open it when it dawned on me that I was still fully dressed. This was bed check! Whirling around, I grabbed my bathrobe from the foot of my bed and threw it on over my clothes. Then I scrambled my hair with my fingers to make it look as if I'd been in bed.

Hurry! I thought frantically. They'll be pounding on the window any second!

I pulled the door open and faked a big yawn. "Hi, Miss Wolfe. We're all here," I said in a dreamy voice.

I started to shut the door again when Miss Wolfe's hand shot out and held the door open. "I must see for myself, you know. It vill only take a second."

I bit my lip as I backed away from the door. I shot a look toward the window as Miss Wolfe peered at Beth's bed. Would she be convinced that Beth was in there? I thought frantically. And could I really hear voices outside, or was it just my imagination?

"Very vell," said Miss Wolfe. "I can see that Beth is sleeping."

Nodding gratefully, I started to open the door again. Maybe I was going to pull this off, after all.

But Miss Wolfe was not moving toward the door to the hall. To my absolute horror, the gym teacher put her hand on the bathroom doorknob. "Your suitemates didn't answer ven I knocked. Instead of using my pass key, I vill just look in from here to make certain everything's okay." With that she marched into the bathroom and disappeared in the darkness.

"Melanie! Open this window!" hissed a voice from outside her room.

I didn't know which way to turn. Should I go with Miss Wolfe and make sure she goes out through George and Bobbi's room? I thought frantically. Or should I stay here and try to signal them to be quiet?

I didn't get a chance to make that decision. A rattling at the window and the frantic cries of Beth made the decision for me.

"Melanie! Open up!"

Beth's muffled voice seemed to fill the room. Had Miss Wolfe heard it? I stuck my head through the drapes and silently mouthed: "GO BACK! I CAN'T OPEN THE WINDOW! MISS WOLFE IS HERE!"

"What are you saying?" yelled George.

"Come on! Open up!" cried Bobbi. "It's freezing out here!"

Behind me, I heard Miss Wolfe marching back through the bathroom. Frantically ducking away from the window, I almost smacked into her in the middle of the room.

"Did I hear voices?" Miss Wolfe asked, frowning.

"Oh . . . um . . . Beth talks in her sleep," I said hastily.

The gym teacher nodded as if she understood and started toward the door. I held my breath. I had to get Miss Wolfe out of here QUICK!

"Actually Beth has talked in her sleep since she was a little kid," I went on. I knew I was talking too fast and too loud, but I had to drown out any sounds that might come from outside. "When we have slumber parties, she always keeps us awake," I rattled on.

"Back to bed now," Miss Wolfe commanded as she finally reached the door. "I vill see you girls in the morning." An instant later she was gone, and I slumped against the door, weak with relief.

Suddenly something thumped against the windowpane. I almost jumped out of my skin. Racing back across the room, I turned the stubborn lock and raised the window as the remnants of a snowball dripped down the pane.

"What's the matter with you?" Beth demanded as she put a leg over the sill and hopped into the room.

"Yeah, you were supposed to let us back in," said George as the other two crawled in after her.

"I was also supposed to be your lookout," I retorted. "And that's just exactly what I *was*! Miss Wolfe was in here doing bed check while you guys were out there hollering to get in."

"Oh, my gosh!" cried Bobbi. "Do you mean to say we almost got caught?"

I nodded. Then I went on to explain about the whole fiasco.

"Wow, I take back what I said about your being chicken," declared George. "It took lots of nerve to do what you did."

Bobbi and Beth said they thought so, too.

"Yeah, but all the trouble started when I fell asleep," I admitted. "I'm so sorry, guys. If I'd stayed awake . . ."

"If you'd stayed awake," George echoed, her eyes twinkling, "we could have eaten this pizza while it was still warm!"

We slapped hands over our mouths to muffle the sound as we burst out laughing.

Now I laughed again at the memory as I looked at the picture of the seventh-grade cheerleading squad in the yearbook. Beth and I had heard from George and Bobbi a couple of times since that hilarious weekend, and the letters had been filled with stories of new practical jokes that George had played with

Bobbi's help. But I had kept the promise I made to myself that night, with Mom and Miss Wolfe on the prowl, and me trying to figure out how to sneak my friends back into the dorm. Since then I had not played another single, solitary practical joke!

CHAPTER

3

*T*hree thousand miles away, in London, England, Christie Winchell's eyes popped open. Her bedroom was pitch-black, and the glowing face of her clock radio announced it was three o'clock in the morning. That made it eight P.M. Wakeman Junior High time.

"I can't believe this. I'm so tuned in to Wakeman's dinner-dance that I woke up in the middle of the night with it on my mind," she mumbled to herself. "I wish I were there."

She closed her eyes again, trying to imagine what her classmates were doing at that very moment. In her mind she could see Wakeman's gym decorated for the biggest night of the year. The tables would be arranged in a horseshoe shape in front of the stage. They would be draped with colored tablecloths and

66

decorated with centerpieces that the dance committee had made.

She imagined cardinal red and gold streamers looped along the gym walls and hanging from the basketball rims. Erase that, she thought with a smile. Jana had written that Shane Arrington was chairman of the decorating committee. He would never go for ordinary crepe paper streamers and balloons. Laser lights and neon light-sticks were more his style.

Right now the gym was probably filling with Wakeman students, including Jana, Katie, Beth, and Melanie—The Fabulous Five minus one. A wave of homesickness rolled over Christie as she imagined her best friends in their new, beautiful dresses. Jana, Melanie, and Katie would be with Randy, Shane, and Tony. Beth had written that she didn't have a date but was going with Alexis and Dekeisha. Christie knew she would be sitting near the other members of The Fab Five. Almost everyone from Wakeman would be there, and all the girls would be dressed to kill.

Shawnie Pendergast's parents had probably bought her the most expensive party dress in town. And Laura McCall would have laid a huge guilt trip on her bachelor dad to get him to shell out big bucks for a gorgeous dress, too.

And the guys! "Ha!" Christie laughed out loud at the thought of them all standing around, looking trapped because they had to wear suits and ties instead of old blue jeans and T-shirts. Clarence Marshall's shirttail would be hanging out from under his suit jacket, and he was probably already a mess from horsing around. She didn't know who Chase Collins's date would be, but he would definitely have one. So would Jon Smith, the other boy she had gone steady with at Wakeman.

More pictures of people at the dance slowly paraded through her mind. Kaci Davis, the ninth-grade queen, would be walking around as if she owned the place. Curtis Trowbridge would be talking to anyone who'd listen about his running for eighth-grade president. It would be so much fun.

A tear suddenly rolled down Christie's cheek. "What's wrong with me?" she grumbled. "I have only a few more weeks left to hang out with Phoebe, Nicki, Eleanore, Connie, and the rest of my British friends. Before I know it, I'll be back in the United States, missing them like crazy."

Christie plumped up her pillow and struggled to a half-sitting position. She was awake now, and memories of the past year crowded out her thoughts of the Wakeman dinner-dance.

Going from Mark Twain Elementary to Wakeman Junior High had been such an adventure. There were so many things to get used to: new friends from Copper Hill and Riverfield elementary schools, new teachers, more demanding classes, going to football and basketball games, hanging out at Bumpers and Taco Plenty—all the things that made junior high school special.

But then, just when I was getting used to Wacko she thought, we moved to London, and my whole life changed. I had to make friends all over again, plus get used to the way British people talk and how they do things.

"I'm a totally different person because of what has happened to me this year," Christie announced to the empty room.

Take boys, for instance. I've actually had three boyfriends this year, she thought, realizing for the first time that none of her friends had dated as many guys this year. Not even Melanie, she added with a smile.

She sank back on her pillow, remembering her very first date. It had been with Jon Smith. "Wow, was I naive then," she whispered. . . .

CHRISTIE'S MEMORY

"Christie, Jon's here," Mom called from the foot of the stairs.

"I'll be right down," I called back.

"How do I look?" I asked the reflection in the bedroom mirror. "Eye shadow not smeared? Check. Lipstick not too heavy? Check. Cologne. *I forgot the cologne!*"

I grabbed my favorite bottle and gave each wrist a small spritz. Then I picked up my brush and ran it through my hair one last time.

"Why am I so nervous?" I asked myself. "We're just going to a movie. It's no big deal. I'll know everyone there."

"Yeah," another part of me answered, "but everyone will stare at you, and they'll probably watch to see if Jon kisses you."

Suddenly I realized I had sprayed both wrists a second time. Frantically I rubbed at them with a tissue. I'd smell up the whole theater!

I opened my bedroom door and headed into the hall. Then I stopped. What if Jon did kiss me? What would it be like to kiss a guy—and then have to face him in school next week?

This is dumb, I thought as I started downstairs. So what if this is my very first date; *I can handle it.*

Jon was standing at the foot of the stairs. When he saw me, he shuffled from one foot to the other, and gave me a weak smile.

He was dressed in black slacks, instead of the worn blue jeans he normally wore to school, and had on a beautiful sweater, but it was the miserable expression on his face that caught my attention.

He looks as if he's going before a firing squad, I thought.

"Hi," Jon greeted me, glancing over his shoulder toward the living room.

I noticed Mom and Dad were sitting in their usual chairs. He was probably checking to see if they were watching.

"You look nice," I said, trying to make him feel more at ease. "I like that sweater."

"Thanks," Jon answered, looking down as if it were the first time he had seen it. "It's uh . . . it's an old one. I don't mean *really* old," he quickly corrected himself. "I just don't wear it very often. I mean, I only wear it on special occasions, like tonight," he corrected himself again.

"That's nice," I replied. I didn't know what else to say. Why were we both so nervous? Ordinarily we talked up a storm.

I grabbed a jacket out of the hall closet and called to my parents, "We won't be late."

"Have fun," my mother called back.

When I reached for the doorknob on the front door, Jon leapt in front of me to grab it. His hand landed smack on top of mine.

"Oops," he said, jerking his hand away. Even though I didn't like the idea of boys' opening doors for girls, I stepped back to let him do it this one time. Somehow that just seemed easier.

"My dad's driving us," said Jon. "There's our car."

No kidding, I thought. It was the only car on the block, and it was parked in front of our house.

Instead of saying what I was thinking, I blurted out, "That's nice." Was that the fourth or fifth time I had said that? I wasn't sure, but I knew I was beginning to sound like a broken record.

Jon was able to open the front door to the car for me without any further fiascos, and I got in next to his father.

"Hi, Christie. How are you?" Mr. Smith asked.

"Fine," I answered, glad that I had finally said something other than "nice."

Suddenly I realized that the car had a center console, and there was room only for the driver and one passenger in front. Jon realized it at almost the same moment. He gave me a weak smile and got in back.

I put my hand over my mouth and cleared my throat to stifle a giggle. I was stuck in the front with his dad, while he was sitting alone in the backseat. This date was definitely not starting off the way I had always dreamed a first date would. I hadn't visualized Jon and me as Scarlett O'Hara and Rhett Butler, but I also hadn't thought we'd both be such total klutzes.

"Let us off at the corner, Dad," Jon said, when we turned into the street in front of Cinema Six.

I mentally applauded Jon for his first smart move of the night. He obviously didn't want the kids in front of the theater seeing him climbing out of the backseat and me getting out of the front. I could just hear Laura McCall and her friends in The Fantastic Foursome making snide remarks.

"Christie! Jon!" called Jana. "Over here."

Jana, Katie, Beth, and Melanie were standing outside the theater with Randy, Tony, Keith, and Shane. We hurried over. I was relieved we'd be with The Fab Five on my first official date with Jon. They'd be around if we ran out of things to say to each other, which was a distinct possibility.

"You'd better get your tickets," Randy told Jon. "The movie starts in five."

"Yeah. If we're going to sit together, we need to get in as soon as the doors open," added Katie.

When Jon went off to get our tickets, Melanie drew me aside. "How's it going?"

I stared at her. "Mel, all we've done is ride here with his father in the car."

Melanie was almost bursting with curiosity. "But did he hold your hand? Has he put his arm around you yet?"

I didn't want to tell her that I had sat in the front and Jon in the back, so he couldn't very well have put his arm around me without practically getting me in a choke hold. I just smiled and said, "No."

When the theater opened, we rushed in, bought popcorn, and found seats halfway down the center section. It was a great location, but it took us forever to decide who would sit next to whom.

After we'd rearranged ourselves a couple of times, I ended up with Jon on my right and Beth on my left. I was glad to have Beth next to me. I could count on her to make conversation.

About twenty minutes into the movie I realized that Jon's arm was touching mine. I glanced at him out of the corner of my eye. He was eating popcorn and staring at the screen, and I couldn't tell if he knew we were touching or not.

Is he giving me a signal? I wondered. Maybe he's going to hold my hand, or put his arm around me.

I didn't know what to do. If I pulled my arm away, he might think I didn't like him. Maybe I should try to let him know it's okay.

Sheesh! I thought. This is my first date, and instead of getting better at it, I'm getting worse!

Just then a movement on my left caught my attention. Keith was holding Beth's hand. I tried not to stare, but I needed to check this kind of thing out. It looked easy. But they've been going together for a long time, I rationalized. It's easy for them; they've got experience.

I sneaked a look around the theater. There were couples all over the place with their heads close together. Some guys had put their arms around the girls, and others probably would soon. Everyone seemed so sure of what to do, and here I was, without a clue.

I wanted to hold Jon's hand, but his eyes were still on the screen, and I couldn't build up the courage to reach out and take his hand. Instead I pressed my arm harder against his, hoping he'd finally notice. Just when I thought he was about to take my hand, he abruptly moved his arm away. He looked at me and mumbled, "Sorry," then stuffed a big handful of popcorn in his mouth.

I could feel myself blushing from top to bottom. What a dumb move I'd made. My first date was turning out to be a total failure. Not only did I not know what I was doing, but Jon didn't seem the least bit interested in me. Why had he bothered to ask me out in the first place? And what would I tell my friends when they asked how it went? I cringed at the thought of Melanie's cross examination, and slumped down in my seat, pretending to watch the rest of the movie.

Jon was quiet when we walked home. I expected him to leave me standing at the door, but instead he looked down at his feet and muttered something so low, I couldn't hear what he said.

"What?" I asked, not really wanting to drag out this nightmare date any more than I had to.

"*I said, I'm sorry you didn't have fun,*" he answered, then turned to leave. "It was my fault."

I was amazed. "Jon, wait!" I cried, grabbing his arm.

"I ruined our date," he said, looking miserable. "I knew all along I would. It's just that I'm such a jerk." He spread his hands in a gesture of frustration. "I don't know what to say."

"You didn't ruin our date, Jon," I said softly. "If it didn't work out, it was my fault, too."

He still looked crestfallen. "But you got stuck in the front seat, and I had to get in the back. Randy or Shane wouldn't have done a stupid thing like that."

"They've dated more than you," I said reassuringly. "I'm sure they were just as nervous on their first dates as you were tonight. Guess what," I added. "I was nervous, too."

"Really?" he asked.

"Of course. Couldn't you tell? The first time you go out with someone is never easy," I told him, trying to sound as if I knew what I was talking about. "It's different from hanging out with a group of kids. All of a sudden you're one-on-one. You really don't know what the other person expects from you."

Jon was smiling as if he was beginning to believe me.

"Look," I said. "Why don't we have our first date over again?"

"Huh?"

"I mean, why don't we go to the movies again soon, and call it our first date?"

His face lit up. "You'll go out with me again? Hey, that's great!"

I smiled at the memory of that night so long ago. My second date with Jon went better—at least the two of us sat together in the backseat of the car on the way to the movies—but I never really thought of him as my boyfriend. We dated for a while longer, then decided to date other people and just be friends. We still are.

I slipped out of bed and went to my desk, turning on the lamp. Inside the top righthand drawer was a box, where I kept a picture of Chase Collins. He was standing on a winners' platform while a judge put a first-place swimming medal around his neck. I sat down in the chair and held the picture under the lamp.

Dating Chase had been completely different, I

thought. He is so handsome and so sure of himself. Because of him I had even broken my curfew a few times and gotten into trouble with my parents. As much as I liked Jon, it was a lot more exciting being with Chase. It'll be only a few more weeks, I realized, until I see him again.

Suddenly I remembered that I'd also be leaving behind Conrad Farrell then. Connie was blond and good-looking, and the son of an English baron. Connie would be a baron himself one day when he was old enough.

He had asked me out several times when I first got to England, but I'd turned him down because of the way I felt about Chase. Besides that, my new friend Nicki McAfee had a crush on him. Gradually I'd realized that I had no idea when I would be going back to the States, and around the same time Nicki had started dating Davey Hopper. One day I'd surprised myself by saying yes when Connie asked me for a date again. Since then we'd spent a lot of time together, and there was one date with Connie that I would never forget.

"That was great!" I said as Connie and I walked Rigel and Buttercup back to the stables. I ran my hand lovingly over Rigel's beautiful black coat.

Rigel was an Arabian horse that I rode whenever I went to the Farrells' country estate in Hoddesdon. He was small, with a dappling of gray on his flanks, and his mane and tail were a creamy white. His humongous brown eyes and delicate face made him look aristocratic.

All of the horses in the stalls that lined both sides of the Farrells' stable were Thoroughbreds. Plaques hanging on the wall of the stable office detailed the horses' royal heritages.

"Cool them down," Connie instructed the stable boy as he handed him Buttercup's reins. "We ran them pretty hard."

Connie took my hand as we walked toward the immense mansion. On the grounds were beautiful formal gardens with colorful rosebushes and rows of hedges that had been neatly shaped into squares and rectangles. Tall statues, some even spouting water, stood at several intersections of the gravel paths. It all seemed so beautiful and magical, I felt like Alice in Wonderland.

"Did you enjoy yourself?" asked Connie's mother as we walked up the concrete steps onto the broad veranda at the back of the house. She and Connie's father were having high tea, which most Britishers did in the late afternoon.

I was awed, as usual, by what Mrs. Farrell was wearing: a beautiful green silk dress, and diamonds sparkling from her ears and fingers. And this was the middle of the day!

Connie's father was wearing a suit jacket and tie, and was sipping tea. He always looked so formal. The front of his jacket was even buttoned. The first thing my father does after work is get rid of his coat.

"We had a great time," I told Mrs. Farrell. "It's a fabulous day."

"Well, sit down and have some tea and sweets," she said. "You must be famished." She turned to the butler. "Neal. Bring two more settings, please."

"I believe you take cream, miss," said Neal as he poured my tea.

"Yes, thank you," I answered politely.

The Farrells were nice, but I had to admit that I was totally intimidated by the fact that they were royalty. I always worried about doing something stupid, and embarrassing myself while I was at their country estate or home in London.

Neal held out a silver tray filled with pastries. I had learned not to take one with my fingers, so I nodded at what I wanted. He used a silver serving knife to put a scone on my plate and then waited patiently while I spread strawberry jam on it. Finally he added a huge dollop of whipped cream.

As Connie and I ate our sweets, I listened to his parents talking.

Mrs. Farrell held up a sheet of paper. "When you have a moment, dear," she told her husband, "I'd appreciate it if you'd look at my guest list to see if there's anyone I've forgotten."

"Umm," he replied, frowning at the names on the list. "It looks all right to me. But why don't we add Christie and her parents? I'm sure you'd like to meet

Prince Charles and Princess Di, wouldn't you, Christie?" he asked, smiling at me.

I almost choked on my pastry. *"Prince Charles? Princess Di?"* I sputtered.

"Yes, dear," said Mrs. Farrell. "Their Majesties will be visiting us, and we're having a reception for them on Saturday. I think it's an excellent suggestion, Harold. Do you think you and your parents can come, Christie?"

I knew my eyes were opened wide in amazement. Me? At a reception for the Prince and Princess of Wales? "Uhh, I . . . we . . ."

"Of course they can come!" Connie answered for me. "Remember, you were telling me that your parents stay home most Saturday evenings, Christie. And you said you didn't have anything planned for then, either, right?"

"Conrad," scolded his mother. "Let Christie make up her own mind." Then she smiled at me. "We would very much like for you to come, dear."

I was so excited, I didn't know what to say. I had watched formal receptions for the Queen of England presented on British television. The ladies were always dressed in formal gowns and dripping with jewelry. The men wore long-tailed tuxedos, and some of them wore colorful sashes to show their royal rank. Some men even wore medals on their chests. A butler called out the names of all the guests as they arrived so everyone knew who they were.

And now I, Christie Winchell, who had never

even had on a formal gown, had the chance to meet top-of-the-line British royalty. It was thrilling . . . but also absolutely terrifying.

"I . . . I guess we can make it," I managed to stutter.

"Good," said Mrs. Farrell. "I'll post an invitation to your parents in the morning. Do tell them we're looking forward to their coming."

Later, as I walked through the foyer to leave, I looked up at the long, winding staircase, where elegantly framed portraits of the Farrell ancestors curved up the wall. I had the feeling they were all looking down at me, wondering what on earth I was doing here.

"Boy, do I envy you, Christie!" exclaimed Phoebe Mahoney a few days later, while she, Eleanore Geach, Nicki McAfee, and I were on a red double-decker bus, riding home from school. Connie was sitting up front with Davey Hopper and Charlie Fenwick, where he couldn't hear us talking. "I've never even seen Lady Di, except on the telly," she went on.

"I've seen Lady Di," said Nicki. "She's just another pretty face. There's no reason to fuss over her." Nothing much ever impressed Nicki.

"How can you say that?" asked Eleanore, looking appalled. "She's gorgeous, and she's going to be the next queen of England."

"She puts her shoes on one at a time, the same as I do," snorted Nicki.

"Her shoes cost about fifty times more than your old sneakers, love," responded Phoebe.

"The truth is, I'm nervous about going to the reception," I admitted. "I won't know how to act. Do I curtsy when I meet Princess Di, the way people do when they meet the Queen? I'll be so scared, I'll probably throw up on those expensive shoes of hers!"

"You'll do fine," said Phoebe. "Just watch what the people in front of you do."

I shook my head resolutely. "No way," I said. "I'm going to be prepared. I'm going to the library after dinner to check out some books on British royalty."

"What are you going to wear?" asked Eleanore.

"Mom and I went shopping at Harrods," I explained, "and I got a beautiful long dress." As my friends tried to reassure me that I'd know what to do around the Prince and Princess, I looked toward Connie. Would he still like me if I made a fool of myself at the reception?

I found two incredibly dull-looking books at the library about British nobility, *Burke's Peerage and Baronetage* and *Debrett's Peerage, Baronage and Companionage*, but both actually turned out to be pretty interesting.

At home I pored over them and found out I was supposed to address both Prince Charles and Lady Di as "Your Highness." According to the charts showing how royal titles related to one another, Mr. Farrell's title of baron put him below a viscount, but above a baronet and knight—which made him seem pretty noble. One funny thing I learned was that knights could belong to something called the Order of the Bath. I could just imagine other knights poking fun at the guys who belonged to that order!

I got more nervous and excited about seeing Princess Di as the days passed. I had learned a few things from the books, but what scared me was the stuff I still didn't know and hadn't the first clue about. I told myself it was ridiculous to be nervous, but that didn't help, nor did my parents.

The reception was all my mother could talk about, and she even took the invitation to show the people at the University of London, where she worked.

Although he tried not to show it, I could tell my father was nervous, too. He rented a tuxedo and fussed about the way it fit. Then he arranged for his company chauffeur, Mr. Finchley, to drive us to Hoddesdon in the company Mercedes-Benz on Saturday instead of us having to show up driving our own car.

Mom and I picked up our dresses on Thursday, and I hurried up to my room to try mine on. I tore open the package and pulled the dress out of the tissue paper Harrods had wrapped it in. It was even prettier than I'd remembered. It was made of pale blue, shimmery satin with a white sash around the waist. The collar was cut square, and the puffed sleeves were trimmed in a delicate white lace.

I quickly slipped out of my school uniform and into the dress. I pulled at the folds in the floor-length skirt to get them to hang just right, then I looked in the mirror. I caught my breath. The dress was beautiful.

I raised my chin, and stood erect the way I thought Princess Di would stand. Then I turned slowly to see myself from every possible direction. Was that really me, Christie Winchell, staring back from the mirror? *Wow*, I thought, *if the kids at Wakeman could only see me now*.

Next I took the sides of the skirt and dipped slowly, putting one foot forward and bending at the waist, the way I remembered seeing women curtsy on television. Should I keep my head up? I wondered, or bow it? I remembered Connie's once telling me how when he was very young, he'd had to go to school to learn manners and how to do things properly. He had laughed and said it was boring, but all kids born into royal families had to do it.

"Mom," I called as I headed for her room.

My mother was just putting her dress away.

"My, you look elegant, Christie."

"Mom, do you know how to curtsy?" I asked. "I mean, the way I'm supposed to at the reception."

"Hmm." She smiled. "I think I can do a reasonable

representation of one." She made a bow that looked a lot like the one I had done.

"Are you sure that's the way they do it in England?" I asked.

She looked puzzled, then laughed. "I really don't think there are many variations, sweetheart. Would you like me to help you practice?"

"Yes!" I immediately answered.

I curtsied for her a couple of times, and she suggested that I keep my head up and my back a little straighter, but that was all. I sighed and thanked her.

You're letting this get totally out of hand, I admitted silently as I took the gown off and carefully hung it in my wardrobe. You have a beautiful dress, you know how to curtsy, and you'll do just fine.

But this isn't a school dance, or a dinner party at your parents' house, a little voice reminded me. British royalty have their own special ways of doing everything.

Saturday evening came long before I was ready for it. As Finchley pulled the car up in front of the Farrells' home, I saw several Rolls-Royces and limousines parked along the long, winding drive.

As I got out of the car, I quickly checked my appearance. My dress looked great, and a quick glance in the car's sideview mirror told me my hair was all right, too.

Neal opened the front door for us. As we stepped inside, Connie's mother swept forward to meet us. "I'm so pleased that you could come," she said, extending her hands to my mother and father. "Christie, you look lovely."

"Thank you for inviting us," my mother replied.

I looked beyond Mrs. Farrell as she and my parents talked. The room was filled with elegantly dressed people. Moving among them were waiters carrying trays filled with glasses and snacks. And then I saw *them*.

Prince Charles and Princess Di were standing together, chatting with several people. He was tall and impeccably dressed, and she was the most beautiful woman I had ever seen. There was something special about the two of them that made them stand out from all the other people around them.

"Come. You must meet Their Highnesses," I heard Mrs. Farrell say. It gradually sank in that she was still talking to my parents, and she meant *we* were going to cross the room and talk to *them*.

Panic streaked through me. I was sure I wouldn't be able to take one step in the Prince and Princess's direction. Then I saw Connie. He had seen me, too, and was smiling. I smiled back and forced myself to follow my parents and his mother.

"Your Highnesses," began Mrs. Farrell as the group surrounding the royal couple parted to let us in. "I'd like to present some friends of ours who have recently moved to London from the United States.

This is Mr. and Mrs. Winchell and their daughter, Christie."

"It's a pleasure to meet you," said the Prince, extending his hand to my father.

I dipped in a small curtsy, and a thrill ran down my spine as Princess Di beamed at me.

She was a tall lady with short blond hair and blue eyes who looked as if she had stepped out of a fashion magazine. She was as elegant and regal-looking as I had always imagined.

"How are you finding your new home, Christie?" the Princess asked. "Have you made new friends?"

"Oh, yes . . . Your Highness," I murmured, suddenly realizing Connie was standing next to me. "Connie . . . Conrad and I are friends, and I've made others at St. Margaret's." I was so nervous, I was almost whispering, but if she noticed, she didn't let on.

"I imagine you miss your friends in the United States," she said sympathetically.

I couldn't believe it. She seemed so kind and concerned about me.

"Oh, yes, I do, but I'm very lucky," I answered with new found courage. "Instead of just The Fabulous Five at home, I've got friends here as well."

"The Fabulous Five?" she echoed. "Who are they?"

I cringed and could feel myself blush. Oh no. Why had I just said that? She'll think this is so babyish. "That's what my friends and I call ourselves," I said, plunging ahead. "We started a self-improvement club when we were in the fifth grade and decided to call ourselves The Fabulous Five. It may sound a little silly, but we really like each other a lot and think we're the best five friends in the whole world. We do everything together. Of course," I added quickly, looking at Connie, "I think my friends here are pretty fabulous, too."

"What a splendid attitude," exclaimed Princess Di. "All young people should try to be the best they can, as you and your friends are doing. It's very commendable."

I blushed all over again. I hadn't meant to sound as if I were trying to score points with her. I hoped that wasn't what she thought.

"Conrad, why don't you take Christie and introduce her to some of the younger people," suggested Mrs. Farrell.

As we walked away, I heard Princess Di say, "You have a perfectly *charming* daughter, Mr. and Mrs. Winchell. She seems so bright and mature."

Connie smiled at me and winked.

During the rest of the party I tried to keep the big grin off my face. I had met the Prince and Princess of Wales, and the Princess had said nice things about me. In fact we talked again later on, and I felt really at ease with her.

What would have made the night entirely perfect was having my friends in The Fabulous Five there, but I wrote them about meeting Lady Di right away.

I couldn't wait for them to spread the word about it back home.

Christie yawned and turned out the desk lamp, then crawled back into bed. Her head was still filled with memories of the past year.

She'd gone all the way from being a total klutz on her first date with Jon Smith, she thought as she pulled up the covers, to meeting the Prince and Princess of Wales. There weren't many kids her age who had curtsied before a princess, and lived on two continents. She'd done some pretty amazing things.

After living in London for almost a year, what will it be like to move back home and go to Wakeman again? Christie wondered. Would the other kids treat her differently? And what would happen between her and Chase? She sighed. It was going to be so hard to say good-bye to Connie. Would they stay in touch next year? She wouldn't know the answers until next year, but if it was anything like this one had been, it would be awesome.

Christie snuggled down in bed and let her imagination take her back to the Wakeman Junior High dinner-dance. A smile crossed her face. She could guess what was happening at this very moment. Mr. Bell was making another long-winded speech.

CHAPTER

$\mathcal{K}$atie Shannon thumbed through *The Wigwam* as she waited for the last round of applause to die down.

"Hey, guys, did you read the seventh-grade class prophecy?" she asked, pointing to a page in the yearbook. "It's terrific. It says here that I'm going to be the first woman president of the United States."

"Oh, look what it says about me!" Melanie cried excitedly.

But before Melanie could read her own prophesy out loud, Mr. Bell cleared his throat and started speaking again.

"This was a year of many new accomplishments at Wakeman Junior High, and one of the most impressive was Teen Court."

There was a sprinkling of applause and a boo from the back of the room. Katie frowned at the boy who was booing. He had been brought before the court a couple of times.

The principal chuckled and went on. "The court replaced the *detention* as a way of keeping law and order at Wakeman, and it also gave you students an opportunity to see our country's court system at work. As you know, the court is made up of nine judges, three each from the ninth, eighth, and seventh grades, and two faculty advisors, Mrs. Brenner and Miss Dickinson. I commend the students who took on the difficult responsibilities of being Teen Court judges. They did an exemplary job and are a credit to the school. Will the two advisors please come up to the podium and introduce your court?"

Katie Shannon felt an unexpected burst of sadness as the two women went forward. This was the last time the nine judges would be together, officially at least. It had been tough to sit in judgment of their fellow students, but it had been rewarding in many ways, too, and even fun.

"I'd like to introduce each of the judges, beginning with the ninth graders, then the eighth graders, and last but not least the seventh graders," began Mrs. Brenner, smiling at the audience. "When your name is called, please come forward. And I'll ask those of you in the audience to please hold your applause until everyone is here."

There was the sound of scraping chairs as the judges prepared to go to the front of the room. Tony nudged Katie and gave her a reassuring smile.

"The ninth-grade judges are Kaci Davis, Kyle Zimmerman, and D.J. Doyle. The eighth graders are Shelly Bramlett, Daphne Alexandrou, and Garrett Boldt. And the seventh-grade judges are Katie Shannon, Shane Arrington, and Whitney Larkin."

Katie raised her head proudly and stood up, taking her place with the others. As Mrs. Brenner and Miss Dickinson began their remarks, Katie's mind flashed back through her year on the court. Mr. Bell was certainly right, not all of their decisions had been easy ones.

She smiled to herself. There had been the time when Randy Kirwan and Keith Masterson had made a casserole out of canned dog food, peas, and cheese and served it to their French class. And the time Tony Calcaterra had been brought before the court by Mr. Naset for wearing an earring to school. That had been a really tough case, since it was then that Katie had first gotten a crush on Tony. But probably the toughest case of all had been the one when she was the head judge and the defendant, Michael Finnerty, had decided to blackmail her. . . .

KATIE'S MEMORY

"I don't see that it makes any difference whether the case belongs before the Court," I announced to everyone in the room. Teen Court was in session, and the judges were debating whether Richie Corrierro and Clarence Marshall should be punished for not returning their cafeteria trays. Mr. Naset, who had been the cafeteria monitor at the time, had filed the complaint.

"Yeah, Katie, but it wasn't any big deal," said Garrett. "Mr. Naset could have just ordered them to go back and get their trays and turn them in. I don't think we should even be hearing this case."

"Richie and Clarence said they only did it because the line was long, and it was too much trouble to wait," added Kaci.

"That's just the point," I said, shaking a finger for emphasis. "I'm not saying I think they *should* be sent before the court, but they *were*, and they did break a rule, so it's our problem now. People can't break rules just because they don't want to be inconvenienced. What if *everyone* ignored the law and did just what they wanted? There'd be criminals running around all over the place."

"All because Richie and Clarence didn't return their cafeteria trays?" snickered D.J. Doyle.

I gave him a dirty look.

"Katie's right," said Mrs. Brenner. "Mr. Naset has made a complaint against the boys. You can find them not guilty, but you must base your decision on more than your feeling that Mr. Naset should have handled the situation differently."

"I think we all agree that Mr. Naset could have taken care of the problem himself," said Shane, who was sitting next to me. "But I agree with Katie that it's our baby now. And, hey, Richie and Clarence admit they did it. So what's to decide?"

I gave Shane a look of appreciation. He was not only laid back, he was smart!

"I guess the only thing we need to decide is what kind of punishment they should get," offered Daphne.

I listened as the others gave in grudgingly. Then we voted for the boys to empty trays from the return into the kitchen for a week. Kyle was acting as bailiff, and he went to get the boys and Mr. Naset, who were waiting in the room next door.

After I read the verdict to them and they left the courtroom, Miss Dickinson suggested that the court recess for five minutes.

"I could use a stretch," admitted D.J. "Hey, Shelly, did I see you put a bag of potato chips in your purse? How about sharing?"

"Get your own," huffed Shelly. "You know where the machines are."

As Shelly and D.J. bickered and the others milled around talking, I decided to make a quick trip to the girls' room.

"Don't be gone long, Katie," called Mrs. Brenner as I started out the door. "We'll be starting again in a couple of minutes."

"Okay," I called back.

I took a few steps down the hallway and stopped. The girls' bathroom was all the way over on the other side of the building. Although school was out for the day and the halls were deserted, it would take me at least five minutes to get there. Even if I ran, I couldn't make it there and back in much less than fifteen minutes.

I turned to go back into the courtroom and stopped again. There was no way I was going to be able to sit through another case without going to the bathroom. And worse yet, since I was the senior judge, if I had an emergency, I would have to stop the trial, excuse myself, and march out of the room with everyone watching. I was embarrassed at the thought.

I glanced toward the boys' bathroom across the hall from where Teen Court was being held. There was probably no one in there. I looked up and down the hall. No one was around. Did I dare?

That's silly, I thought. I can't possibly go into the boys' bathroom. But the ache in my bladder told me I'd better decide what to do quickly.

I tiptoed over to the door and opened it a few inches. "Is anyone in there?" I called in a tiny voice.

No one answered.

Throwing a last quick glance over my shoulder, I stepped in cautiously before I could lose my nerve.

"Anyone in here?" I said in a louder voice.

When there was still no answer, I bit my lip and looked for feet under the stall doors. I was in luck, so I picked a stall and used it. The thud in my chest was starting to subside when I washed my hands. Another couple of minutes and I'd be back in the courtroom—home free.

Just then the door squeaked behind me. I shot a look in the mirror, and to my horror I was looking straight into the eyes of an eighth grader named Michael Finnerty!

We stared at each other for an instant. Then Michael's face turned crimson and he looked confused—as if he had gone into the wrong place. But as he turned to leave, he seemed to realize that it wasn't *his* problem. He hadn't gone into the *girls' bathroom* by mistake. He flashed me a sly grin.

"I . . . uh, I was in a hurry," I spluttered, aware that my face was probably as red as my hair. "I have to get back to Teen Court. The girls' bathroom, uh . . . is so far away and . . ."

His grin got bigger—and slyer—and I rushed past him and streaked out the door.

I stopped in the hall to recover my composure before going into the courtroom again. I had never been so embarrassed in my entire life. And what made it worse, Michael would probably tell *everyone* at Wakeman that he had caught Katie Shannon using the boys' bathroom!

Taking a deep breath, I went back into the courtroom. The other judges had taken their places and were getting ready for the next case. I hurried to my seat, eager to get this day over with and go home.

"We're ready," announced Miss Dickinson. "Kyle, would you bring in the next defendant and complainant, please?"

As we waited for them to enter, I took a few deep breaths and felt a little better.

But when the door opened, I looked up to see Michael Finnerty following Kyle into the courtroom with Mr. Neal, an English teacher, right behind him.

Michael gave me a big smile, and I wanted to die on the spot.

While Kyle showed Michael and Mr. Neal where to sit, D.J. brought up Richie and Clarence's case again.

"I still think we shouldn't hang someone for doing something that's no big deal," D.J. insisted.

"We didn't hang them," countered Daphne. "They broke a rule, and they knew it. As Katie says, you can't just break a rule because obeying it is too much trouble."

"I agree with D.J.," said Kaci. "It bothers me that we had to punish them at all."

"Well, I think Katie was right," said Shelly. "You can't just go around breaking rules and expect to get away with it."

While they were debating, I glanced toward Michael. He was listening attentively to the conversation. I looked away before he saw me and smirked at me again.

"It's time to get on with the next case," said Mrs. Brenner.

I cleared my throat, straightened my shoulders, and tried to look official. "Shelly, would you read the charge, please?"

"The next plaintiff is Mr. Neal," announced Shelly, who was the court's clerk for the day. "He has filed a complaint against Michael Finnerty, charging him with taking Billy Peterson's English homework. Mr. Neal says Michael took Billy's homework at least once before, and was reprimanded for doing it then."

"Do you have anything to add to the charge, Mr. Neal?" I asked.

"Yes, Your Honor," replied Mr. Neal. "Michael got hold of Billy's homework on the way to school. Michael claims that he took it so he could write down the assignment, but he kept it the entire day, and Billy didn't have a chance to finish it. I have to add, there was a great similarity between the answers on Billy's and Michael's papers when they were turned in. Both students used very similar wording in their answers."

"Did Michael take the homework, or did Billy give it to him?" asked Garrett.

"Actually, that's a point of confusion," said Mr. Neal. "At first Billy said Michael took it. Later he said he let Michael have it. I'm not sure, although I have my suspicions."

I took notes on the pad of paper in front of me. I had dreaded the moment when I had to look Michael in the eye, but I couldn't avoid it any longer. "Michael Finnerty, do you have a response to these charges?"

Michael stood up. "Yes, Your *Honor*."

Was there another smirk on Michael's face? I couldn't be sure.

"I lost my notes from the day before," Michael explained. "All I wanted was to see what our assignment was. I thought Billy was my friend and wouldn't mind."

"Why did he say at first that you took the homework?" asked Kaci.

Michael shrugged and smiled. "Fuzzy thinker, I guess."

"Why did you keep the homework all day?" asked

Shane. "Why didn't you just ask Billy what the assignment was and write it down?"

"Didn't have time," muttered Michael. "Bell was about to ring."

"I thought you took the homework on the way to school," said Kaci. "It sounds as if you should have had time."

"I had other stuff to do," answered Michael, frowning. "I was in a hurry. I was going to give it back. It wasn't as if I was cheating or anything."

"Mr. Neal said your answers were a lot like Billy's," challenged Kyle. "How do you account for that?"

"Mr. Neal said the answers were *similar*," said Michael, looking contritely at his teacher. "He didn't say they were the same. If there's a right answer, how many ways are there to say it that don't sound similar?"

Kyle looked at Michael speculatively and then turned to Mr. Neal. "Would you care to respond to what Michael is saying?"

"Yes, I would," replied Mr. Neal. "Number one, Michael has English class during the last period of the day. Even if Michael had only wanted to copy the assignment, he had ample time to do it and return Billy's paper to him. Number two, I've seen many answers that were correct, but phrased in distinctively different ways. Michael's answers were *too* similar to Billy's. And number three, I think Billy was telling the truth the first time. I definitely believe he wasn't happy about Michael's taking the homework."

"Where is Billy, anyway?" I asked.

"I don't know," said Mr. Neal. "I was hoping he'd be here."

"Hey, can I help it if Billy got upset because I kept his homework longer than I should have?" protested Michael. "I'm sorry about that, but I didn't break any rules, *like some people do*." My heart stopped. He was looking straight at me as he said it. "I heard you guys talking, and you said people can't just break a rule because obeying it is too much trouble. *I* would *never* do a thing like that, but some people would."

He gave me a crafty little smile. I knew what was coming next, but there was nothing I could do to stop it.

"You know . . . like some guys might want to use the girls' bathroom just because the boys' room is too far away, and they're in a hurry. It could happen to a girl, too, but you wouldn't catch me doing anything like that."

Heat rushed up my neck, turning my face bright red. I held my breath, waiting for him to tell the entire court about catching me in the boys' room.

"Of course," he continued casually, "sometimes you shouldn't judge people too quickly." His eyes flicked toward me for an instant, and I understood what was happening. "Not if *you've* broken a rule yourself, and maybe no one knows about it. If someone found out, you'd look really bad."

My entire body was on fire now, and I barely heard Shane ask, "What does that have to do with anything? Nobody here has broken any rules, except maybe you."

Michael's sly grin was back, and he didn't say anything.

I forced my mind back to my job as senior judge. "Do any of the other judges have questions for Michael or Mr. Neal?" I asked in a tiny voice.

No one did.

"Then we'll consider the evidence," I announced. "Mr. Bailiff." I turned to Kyle. "Would you escort Michael and Mr. Neal to the waiting room, please?"

I watched Kyle lead them out of the room. Maybe Shane and the others didn't understand the message Michael had been trying to deliver, but I certainly did. He had been threatening to blackmail me.

"Michael had a point," said Kyle. "If the answer to a question is 'A rock rolls downhill because of gravity,' how many ways are there to say that? There's no way of knowing for sure that Michael copied Billy's homework. And we can't convict him without absolute proof."

"It seems pretty clear to me," countered Kaci.

"Michael's a bully, and he took Billy's homework to copy it. Everyone knows that Michael pushes other people around."

"I don't know that," said Daphne. "And besides, can we convict him just because he may have done something in the past?" She looked at Mrs. Brenner and Miss Dickinson for advice.

"Good thinking, Daphne," commented Miss Dickinson. "Whether a person's record can be considered during a trial is argued before the civil courts all the time. In most cases they won't allow it. You have to consider the evidence in front of you."

For twenty minutes I listened to the other judges argue about whether or not Michael was guilty. I was totally confused. Was he guilty or not? Part of me said he was. But part of me said you couldn't convict someone on circumstantial evidence. If Billy had been there to testify, things might have been different. Had Michael *forcibly* taken Billy's homework and then copied his answers? How could we know for sure?

But something else was bothering me, too. Had Michael really been threatening me, or had I just imagined it? Was I just so embarrassed about being caught in the boys' bathroom that I expected him to get revenge if Teen Court found him guilty?

"I think it's time we took a vote," said Mrs. Brenner. "We can't keep Michael and Mr. Neal waiting all evening."

I took a deep breath. This was it. We would have to find him either guilty or not guilty.

I looked down the long table. "Garrett, how do you find Michael Finnerty?"

Garrett rubbed his forehead and frowned. "I find him . . . not guilty."

I wrote down Garrett's name and his vote.

"Shelly, how do you find Michael Finnerty?" I asked.

"I find him guilty," she answered without hesitation.

I repeated the question to each judge, and my spirits sank as I recorded their votes. Daphne, Whitney, and D.J. voted not guilty, and Shane, Kaci, and Kyle voted guilty. It was a tie, and since I was the senior judge, my vote would be the tiebreaker. Everyone was looking at me.

Why did it have to be me, of all people? I thought miserably. And why did Michael have to catch me in the boys' restroom?

I tried to think about the evidence. After all, I was a judge and I believed in justice. Unfortunately it wasn't a clear-cut case. The tie vote proved that. It had been wrong for Michael to take Billy's homework, but maybe he really had lost his assignment. It happened all the time. It had even happened to me, and I had had to call a friend. And there wasn't any real proof that he had copied the answers. Was he guilty or not guilty?

"Well, Katie?" said Mrs. Brenner. "Yours is the last vote. How do you find Michael?"

I looked from one judge to the other, and they were looking back expectantly. What could I do? I had to be fair. But then a vision of Michael smiling at me in the mirror in the boys' room flashed into my mind.

My mouth went dry. "Not guilty," I said barely above a whisper.

"I'm surprised about the way you voted, Katie," Shelly told me as we walked home together. "Especially after your big speech about not breaking rules. Michael could have called Billy the night before and gotten the assignment. It's pretty obvious to me that he just took Billy's homework and copied the answers."

I glanced at her nervously out of the corner of my eye. "It's just the way I saw it. You can't convict someone unless there's positive proof."

Shelly shrugged. "Michael took Billy's homework once before. It'll be interesting to see if he does it again. See you tomorrow," she said, turning down a side street.

I felt depressed as I walked on by myself. I had voted the right way, hadn't I? There wasn't any positive proof. And the fact that Michael had been a bully before couldn't be counted. Then I remembered the look on Shane's face when I voted. He had been surprised. Actually he had been more than surprised. He had been shocked. But just because we were friends and respected each other's opinions didn't mean we agreed on everything.

Still I couldn't erase the memory of Michael's knowing smile when the verdict was read. It was obvious he thought he had intimidated me and affected the outcome of the trial.

I stopped in the middle of the sidewalk. Is that what really happened? Was I kidding myself into thinking I had made a fair decision based on the evidence? Or had I really voted not guilty because I was afraid Michael would tell on me for being in the boys' bathroom?

I started getting sick to my stomach. Had I—Katie Shannon, who was committed to justice for all— sold out? If I had, I would never be able to forgive myself. There was only one thing to do. I had to find out once and for all if Michael Finnerty was guilty or not.

The next morning at school I looked everywhere for Billy. Finally I spotted him. He and Michael were standing by the bike rack and talking. They seemed to be getting along okay. Later I saw Billy ahead of me in the hall, and I hurried to catch up with him.

"Hi, Billy," I said, trying to sound casual. "How's it going?"

"Oh, hi, Katie. Okay, I guess."

I bit my lip. It was now or never. "Uh, Billy, can I ask you something?"

Billy shook his head. "Can it keep? I've got a test first period, and I can't be late."

"It'll only take a second," I insisted, pulling him out of the milling crowd. "You know Mr. Neal took Michael Finnerty to Teen Court yesterday, right?"

"Yeah, I know," said Billy, looking down at his shoes.

"Billy, did you lend Michael your homework, or did he take it?" I asked in my most serious voice.

I thought I saw a look of panic flash across his face.

He glanced away. "I lent it to him," he mumbled.

"First you told Mr. Neal that Michael took it. Then you changed your story. How come?" I asked.

Billy eyed me tensely. "Look, the Teen Court said Michael was innocent. That's all there is to it."

I looked at him closely, but he avoided my eyes. "Are you sure that's all there is to it?" I pressed.

"That's what I said, isn't it?" He moved away. "I've got to get to class."

I watched him disappear down the hall. My gut feeling that I had voted the wrong way was growing.

"If you want to change your vote to guilty, why don't you tell Mrs. Brenner or Miss Dickinson?" asked Melanie. The Fab Five were sitting in a booth at Bumpers.

"I can't," I explained. "The trial's over. I think that would be what they call double jeopardy, trying someone twice for one crime."

"Does Teen Court actually pay attention to all that legal stuff?" asked Beth.

I nodded. "Mrs. Brenner and Miss Dickinson want us to go by the law. It's the only way to be fair."

"Well, it doesn't seem fair to me," commented Jana. "If Michael really did take Billy's homework, he shouldn't get off free."

"I don't know what you can do, Katie, with Billy backing down on his original story," said Beth. "I'll bet it's because he's afraid of Michael."

"If Christie were here, she'd be able to figure out what to do," remarked Melanie with a sigh. "She's so brainy."

"Yeah, but Christie's not here," I pointed out gloomily.

Jana nudged me. "There's Billy over by the jukebox."

I glanced up. Billy was standing by himself, selecting a song. The minute I looked at him, Michael walked up and put an arm around Billy's shoulder. At first Billy seemed to panic, but then Michael gave his arm a friendly punch and left. Billy's shoulders sagged, and he angrily poked at the buttons to play a song.

"Did you see that?" asked Beth. "I wonder what Michael said to him?"

I narrowed my eyes angrily. Being brought before Teen Court hadn't scared Michael one bit. He had been harassing Billy and smiling while he was doing it. He had a lot of nerve thinking he could get away with bullying anybody, especially Billy Peterson!

Who am I kidding? I thought, sinking back in my seat in defeat. He intimidated me, didn't he? And I'm a Teen Court judge. How can I blame Billy for backing down? And what do I think I can do about it?

"If I could just talk Billy into being a witness against Michael," I muttered, half to myself.

"Forget it," advised Melanie. "He's too scared."

I nodded, but a plan was taking shape in my mind. "I think just maybe I know what to do," I said, motioning my friends in closer. "Listen to this . . ."

"Well, look who's here: Katie, Jana, Beth, and Melanie," said Mr. Neal. "I don't see much of you girls anymore. How are you?"

We all smiled and murmured hello. Mr. Neal had been our fifth-grade teacher at Mark Twain Elementary before he was transferred to Wacko. I looked at Jana out of the corner of my eye. She was blushing. It was because she used to have a crush on him at Mark Twain, and she always called him *dreamy* Mr. Neal.

"We were wondering if you could help us with something," I began.

"I'll be happy to, if I can," he responded. "Shoot."

I quickly explained my predicament—blushing when I got to the part about Michael's catching me in the boys' bathroom—and then told him my plan. The expression on his face went from mildly interested to very serious. When he started nodding, I knew that he would help.

The next morning I met Melanie, Beth, and Jana at a corner a few blocks from school.

"Remember," I instructed, "it's important that he doesn't see us following Billy."

"I know," Beth said excitedly. "Just like in the movies. I follow him for a block, then Melanie follows him a block."

"And I'll be waiting to follow him the next block," finished Jana.

"Right," I said. "I'll stay completely out of sight. If Michael sees me, he'll be suspicious and won't do anything."

My friends and I fanned out, and I took up my position behind a tree. I had hidden my bicycle in the shrubbery in front of an apartment building.

I crossed my fingers for luck and stole a peek around the tree. Melanie was standing on the corner, trying to look as if she were waiting for someone. Lots of kids passed her on the way to school and a few nodded and said hello.

"Hi, Mel. Waiting for someone?" asked Dekeisha when she and Marcie Bee came by.

"Oh, uh, yeah," spluttered Melanie.

"If it's Katie, she's behind that tree," Marcie told her, giggling. "I think she's playing a trick on you."

I almost died, and Melanie looked flustered.

Thinking quickly, I whispered loudly, "We're playing a trick on someone else. Please act as if you haven't seen me. Okay?"

"How could anybody miss you?" said Dekeisha, rolling her eyes. "Your skirt's sticking out."

I gulped and looked down. "Oh!" The stiff material of my brand-new denim skirt stuck out a mile. "Thanks," I said sheepishly.

"Lots of luck, Pink Panther," called Marcie as she and Dekeisha walked away.

"Uh-oh, here comes Billy," said Melanie, quickly striking her pose again.

I lunged back behind my tree and gathered my skirt in close to my legs. Holding my breath, I dared another peek. Billy hadn't seen me.

He barely glanced at Melanie as he passed her, and she waited a moment and then fell in step several yards behind him.

I watched until it was safe. Then I grabbed my bike and rode like mad around the block. When I turned the last corner, Billy had already reached the next block, and Michael was nowhere in sight. Just like clockwork, Beth fell in behind Billy, and Melanie crossed the street and joined Heather Clark. What a surveillance team! I thought, and smiled to myself. Billy didn't suspect a thing.

I spun my bike and headed around the next block, pedaling harder this time to keep Billy from getting too far ahead of me. When I got close enough to see again, Beth was crossing over to Melanie and Heather, and Jana was waiting for Billy to get far enough ahead for her to start her part of the spy mission.

I bit my lip. Still no Michael. Maybe I had guessed wrong about what he would do after Mr. Neal kept his end of the bargain. The closer we got to school, the less likely it was that Michael would try anything.

That instant I saw Michael appear from behind a big tree and stop Billy. He looked casual until Jana passed, and then he grabbed Billy and pulled him behind the tree.

I laid my bicycle gently to the ground. Ducking low, I scooted along behind a hedge, getting close enough to hear what was going on. I peered over the hedge and signaled Beth and Melanie to be careful, because they had left Heather, and were headed my way, as planned. Still their timing had to be just right, or our scheme wouldn't work.

I turned my attention back to Michael and Billy.

"I'll give it back after homeroom this time," promised Michael.

"That's what you said the last time," grumbled Billy.

Keeping my ears tuned to Billy and Michael's conversation, I checked my friends. Melanie and

Beth were pretending to look through Beth's back-pack, but it was obvious that they were listening, too. Jana was circling back to join Melanie and Beth. The boys wouldn't think anything of that, if they noticed, since the three girls were best friends.

Now Michael's voice turned hard. "Are you call-ing me a liar, Billy Peterson?"

Billy shook his head. "Maybe you forgot last time, but I can't lend it to you this time. Mr. Neal gave us a double assignment yesterday, and I didn't get a chance to finish it last night. I need to work on it, so why don't you just copy down the assignment?"

Michael sounded angry now. "Look, Peterson, do you want your lights punched out?"

Billy hesitated an instant and then thrust a paper toward Michael. "Here, take it. But give it back after homeroom, like you promised."

"Hey, don't worry," assured Michael, grinning. "We're friends, aren't we? I'll get it back to you, right after lunch."

"You said homeroom." Billy's voice sounded pan-icky.

I couldn't wait any longer. I clenched my fists and stepped out of my hiding place. "I can't believe you, Michael Finnerty! You're nothing but a big bully!"

Michael's mouth dropped open in surprise. "Wha . . ."

"Don't deny it," said Jana. "I heard what you said."

"We did, too," chimed in Beth, motioning toward Melanie.

Michael gave us each a surly look. When he looked at me, his expression changed a little. I knew what he was thinking, but I didn't care. "When Mr. Neal hears about this, you're going to be in big trouble."

Michael smirked. "Oh, yeah? And who's going to tell him? Are you, Billy?"

He stared hard at Billy, and Billy backed away, shaking his head.

"Billy," I argued, "we heard the whole thing. He won't hurt you if you turn him in."

Billy shrugged and looked at the ground. "I . . . I don't want to. It's just homework. It's no big deal."

"No big deal," cried Jana. "Don't you know that he'll never leave you alone until you stand up to him?"

Billy shrugged.

"Hey, Billy and I are friends, okay?" said Michael, putting a brotherly arm around Billy's shoulders.

Billy looked uncomfortable, but he didn't say anything.

My blood was starting to boil, and I clenched my teeth to stay in control. Billy was such a coward. Part of me wanted to shout at him that it was his own fault for being in such a mess. But justice still had to be done, and shrugging the whole thing off by saying it was Billy's own fault meant Michael would get away with cheating on his homework.

I looked Michael straight in the eye and said in a level voice, "If Billy doesn't turn you in, I will."

A sly grin spread over Michael's face. "You do that, Katie, and I'll tell the whole school about catching you in the boys' bathroom. There may not be a rule in the student handbook against it, but everybody knows you're not supposed to do it." He paused and watched my face turning crimson. "You'll be in worse trouble than I am, because you're a judge on Teen Court. Judges are the last people who can break rules. I bet they'd kick you off the court."

I stared at him in shock. I had never thought about being kicked off the court. Could he be right? It did make sense. How could I break rules and then hand out punishment to other kids?

I looked at Michael. His air of superiority was sickening. I drew in my breath and made a decision.

"I don't care, Michael Finnerty. I'm going to turn you in, anyway. You're a bully, and you need to be punished for what you've been doing to Billy and for cheating on your homework."

Michael looked at me in surprise. Then his eyes narrowed. "You're nuts if you do, Katie Shannon."

"I'll see you in court," I scoffed.

"Wow, Katie. Are you really going to turn Michael in?" asked Melanie when The Fab Five had gathered at the school fence a few minutes later.

"I don't have a choice now," I replied glumly. "If I don't, Michael will think I'm afraid of him, and he'll keep on bullying people—me included!"

"Your giving up Teen Court would be like my giving up acting," Beth observed sympathetically. "I don't know if I could make that kind of sacrifice."

"It won't be the end of the world," I said, smiling weakly. I didn't want them to know how worried I was, so I added, "And, hey, it won't keep me out of law school."

"Darn that Billy, anyway," said Jana. "You were only trying to protect him. If he had the guts to turn Michael in, Michael might not tell on you."

"Don't count on it," I said. "Even if Michael doesn't turn me in to Teen Court, he's so mad at me that I know he'll spread it all over school that I used the boys' bathroom."

Gloom settled over the four of us.

Later that day I stopped by Mr. Neal's room.

He looked up from the papers he was grading. "Hi, Katie. How did everything go with Michael and Billy? Did my giving extra homework flush out our criminal?" he asked, smiling.

I took a deep breath and started telling him how the rest of The Fab Five and I had worked our trap.

"What's the next case, Shelly?" asked Kyle Zimmerman. He was senior judge for the day, and Shelly Bramlett was court clerk.

"Michael Finnerty is the defendant, and Mr. Neal is the plaintiff . . . again," reported Shelly. "Also, Katie and Billy Peterson are witnesses."

The other judges looked at Katie questioningly.

"Mrs. Brenner, Miss Dickinson, I think I need to step down as a judge," I said.

Miss Dickinson nodded. "If you're going to be a witness, you must."

I left the judges' table and took a seat at a nearby table with Beth, Jana, and Melanie, who had come to court to offer testimony if it was needed. It seemed odd to be facing the court. The judges all looked so solemn and proper, not in the least the way they looked most of the time.

"Daphne, would you please get Michael and Mr. Neal?" asked Kyle.

I gripped my hands in tight fists as I waited for the bailiff to bring them in. This had to be it. The moment I had dreaded. Amazingly, no one this past week had mentioned hearing that I had used the boys' bathroom. Apparently Michael hadn't told anyone yet. It could only mean that he was waiting to drop the bombshell during Teen Court. Of course that would make it even more sensational.

Mr. Neal had worked hard to convince Billy to be a witness, even though The Fab Five had all seen Michael bullying him. I hoped he wouldn't lose his nerve when he took the stand.

The door opened, and Daphne entered, followed by Michael and Mr. Neal. They took seats at a table nearby, and Michael glared at me. I closed my eyes and took a deep breath, telling myself that this was not going to be one of the worst moments of my life. I had to do it. There was no other way.

I forced myself to open my eyes again. Then I raised my hand. "May I say something to the court before the hearing starts?" I asked.

Miss Dickinson frowned at me over the top of her wire-frame glasses. "If it has to do with the complaint against Michael, I'm afraid not. We have to follow procedure."

"It doesn't," I said firmly. "It has to do with something I did."

Everyone in the room stared at me. I could feel myself blushing, but I couldn't let my embarrassment keep me from doing the right thing, no matter how much I dreaded it.

Slowly I got to my feet, then cleared my throat. When I began to speak, I could barely hear my own words over the pounding of my heart. "At the last session of Teen Court, I left the room to go to the girls' restroom. You said to hurry, Mrs. Brenner, so instead of going all the way to the other side of the building to the girls' room, I . . . I went into the boys' room."

Mrs. Brenner looked surprised. Kyle and D.J. snickered. And Kaci covered her mouth to hide her smile. All of the judges, except Shane, started whispering to each other. Only Michael had a look of disbelief on his face.

And these are my friends, I thought. Imagine when everyone else hears about it. They'll have a ball at my expense.

"Why are you bringing this up, Katie?" asked Mrs. Brenner, looking puzzled.

"Because it was the wrong thing to do, and I wanted to be the one to tell." I glanced at Michael. He looked as if the rug had been pulled out from under him. For the first time in a week I wanted to smile.

"I'm the one who believes people shouldn't break rules just because it's inconvenient to obey them," I continued. "I broke a rule, and I want the court to decide on a punishment for me."

Now all the judges were staring at me.

Mrs. Brenner was totally discombobulated. "Oh, my," she murmured.

"You've got to," I insisted. "Last week we punished Richie and Clarence for breaking a rule that was inconvenient. I can't be treated any differently just because I'm on Teen Court."

Suddenly all the judges began talking at once, and the two faculty advisors looked at each other.

"Katie also doesn't want to be blackmailed," said Billy, standing up. Now everyone looked at him. "I guess it's true that Michael Finnerty walked in on Katie in the boys' room. I don't know, but I heard him tell her that she'd better not tell Mr. Neal about taking my homework or he'd tell everyone about what she did."

Billy's voice was getting stronger, and confidence was shining in his eyes. "It's not fair for her to take all this heat just because I wouldn't stand up to Michael. If it's okay, I'd like my name put on the complaint, or whatever it's called, as the one who's accusing Michael of taking my homework. It was the fifth time he did it. You just didn't know about the other times."

I blinked at Billy. He wasn't a coward anymore. I couldn't restrain myself and started applauding Billy. The rest of The Fab Five applauded, too.

"Order in the court!" commanded Kyle, rapping his gavel on the table. Appearing confused, he looked to the advisors for help.

"We need a moment for the court to confer, don't you agree, Elizabeth?" Mrs. Brenner asked Miss Dickinson.

"Definitely. Daphne, would you take everyone into the hall while the judges talk this over, please?"

Daphne led The Fab Five and me, Mr. Neal, Michael, and Billy into the hall. My friends and I gathered away from the others. Michael stood on one side of the hall, looking furious. Billy stood on the other side, staring at the floor and looking miserable. Mr. Neal busied himself with some papers in his briefcase.

"Boy, you blew their minds, Katie," Beth whispered, grinning. "I love it. You ruined Michael's big plan to embarrass you, and you've got the judges so confused that they don't know what to do."

"I like ruining Michael's plan, but I'd rather not have the judges in there talking about what to do to me," I confessed, watching Billy. I felt sorry for him. He looked so nervous. It had taken a lot of courage on his part to stand up to Michael in the courtroom.

"Excuse me a minute, guys," I said. "I'll be right back."

I went to Billy. "Hi," I said.

He looked at me and then down at the floor. "Hi," he mumbled.

"I want you to know that I think you were very brave in there," I told him.

He gave me a lopsided little smile. "Big deal. When you told on yourself, I realized what a total coward I'd been. If I had admitted to Mr. Neal that Michael was harassing me into giving him my homework, you wouldn't be in all this trouble. I'm sorry."

I reached out and touched his arm. "Thanks, but he would have told on me sooner or later. He was just saving his secret to hang over my head. I don't know for sure, but I have a feeling the reason I voted to let him off last time was that I was afraid of him. If that's true, I wasn't very brave, either. The important thing is how it all turns out."

Billy's smile looked more relaxed. "I hope the court isn't too tough on you."

In a few minutes Daphne stuck her head out the door. "You can all come back in now."

When everyone was seated, Kyle rapped his gavel for attention. "The court will come to order."

He paused while we all got settled. "We have two things before us today: the complaint by Mr. Neal against Michael Finnerty, and Katie's request that the court consider her, uh . . . what's the word Miss Dickinson used . . . infraction? Anyway, that she shouldn't have gone into the boys' bathroom."

My heart was beating triple time. I looked at the judges, trying to guess what they had decided. I couldn't help wondering what I would have recommended if I had been one of them.

Kyle continued. "First we'll take up Katie's request."

I tensed and my mouth went dry as Kyle looked down at his notes.

"The court has decided," Kyle said slowly, "that since a complaint has not been filed against Katie, we have no, uh . . ." he referred to his notes again, "*grounds* to hear the case. Until *someone* files a complaint," Kyle went on, looking at Michael, "there can't be a hearing."

My heart jumped into my mouth. I couldn't believe it. They weren't going to punish me, after all. I blinked back tears of joy as I looked at my smiling friends.

Michael slid down in his chair under stern stares from Garrett and D.J. Shane winked at me. He knows as well as I do that Michael won't dare file a complaint against me, I thought.

"Now, about the complaint filed against Michael

by Mr. Neal," continued Kyle. "Michael, do you have anything to say in your own defense?"

Michael shook his head sullenly.

"In that case," concluded Kyle, "the court finds you guilty and sentences you to three weeks of helping Mr. Bartosik clean blackboards and empty trash cans after school. Court is now dismissed until next Friday."

I told my friends I'd meet them in the hall and waited until everyone had cleared the courtroom. Then I walked slowly to the judges' table and sat down. It felt good to sit there again. It felt even better to know that justice had finally been done. And in that special moment I promised myself that I would never let someone blackmail me into doing something I knew was wrong. And I would never, *never*, *NEVER* use the boys' bathroom again!

CHAPTER

5

"Before I introduce the final organization to you this evening," said Mr. Bell, stepping up to the microphone again, "I would just like to say that while including a report card for teachers in the yearbook was a very clever idea, I would personally like to protest the C you gave me for my hairstyle."

Beth Barry glanced quickly at the principal. Was he angry? His big smile told her instantly that he wasn't, and she breathed a sigh of relief.

Mr. Bell patted the shiny bald spot on the top of his head and went on. "Actually, I don't believe that I have enough hair to get any grade whatsoever for hairstyle."

The kids went wild, laughing and applauding.

Even Crazy Reggie Robards stood and clapped his hands.

Mr. Bell laughed good-naturedly with the crowd. When everyone had settled down again, he cleared his throat and said, "I have a little secret to share with you at this time. In case you haven't noticed, Tim Riggs, a member of Wakeman's new Media Club, has been filming the awards presentations and the recognition of school activities with the club's camcorder. The video will be shown on our school's own television program, *The Wakeman Bulletin Board*, this Saturday morning on the local cable station."

There were lots of oooohs and ahhhhs around the room, and Tim stepped from the shadows near the stage and took a bow.

"Now, to tell you a little bit more about the Media Club and *The Wakeman Bulletin Board*, here is our fine drama coach and faculty advisor, Mr. Levine."

Beth raised halfway out of her chair and clapped as hard as she could. This was the moment she had been waiting for—her last chance to be a seventh-grade star.

When Mr. Levine read the role call of Media Club members, Beth hurried to the stage to take her place beside Shawnie Pendergast, Funny Hawthorne, Shane Arrington, Jon Smith, and Paul Smoke. At the last minute Tim Riggs handed the camcorder to Curtis Trowbridge so Curtis could continue shooting while Tim joined the others on the stage.

When all the names had been read aloud, the club members bowed low.

I love being in the spotlight, Beth thought, feeling her pulse race at the sound of her classmates' applause. At least most of the time I do, she mused. But there was one time when she almost gave up performing forever. She felt heat creep up her neck as she remembered the occasion. . . .

BETH'S MEMORY

"Hey, everybody. There's a big countywide basketball tournament starting next week. Does anybody have any great ideas for promoting it on this week's show? We want everybody rooting for Wakeman," said Funny. It was her month to be the show's director, and she liked to get things organized as early as possible.

"You mean, start a little *hoop*-la?" I asked, wiggling my eyebrows and grinning.

Shane shook his head. "Bizarre, Barry. You're totally bizarre."

"I know, but I'm lovable," I quipped back, and everyone laughed.

"I'm serious, guys," said Funny. "The tournament's a big deal, and I hate for the co-anchors to just read an announcement. We need something interesting to stir up some school spirit."

"We could interview a couple of Wakeman players," offered Shawnie.

"That would take too long," Paul pointed out. "The whole show's only fifteen minutes long, and we've got a lot of other things to talk about besides."

"Anyway, it would sound too staged," added Funny. "What we need is something that will really get kids' attention."

Suddenly a light flashed on in my brain. My idea would get kids' attention, all right, and it would be a riot. I thought about it for another split second. It was too good—too *perfect*—to pass up.

Smiling slyly, I said, "Leave everything to me, troops. I have just the thing to make our whole audience sit up and take notice."

"Great. What is it?" asked Funny.

"You'll see," I promised.

"But I'm the director," Funny insisted. "I have to know if it's appropriate, how much time it takes, stuff like that. You know that, Beth."

I gave her my most mysterious smile. "Trust me."

I flew home after the meeting and headed down to the basement. It took a little digging, but I finally found my brother Brian's sixth-grade Halloween costume in an old packing box in a corner. He had been almost the same size in sixth-grade as I was in seventh, so I knew it would fit. "Wait till they see me in this!" I cried as I pulled the round, orange papier-mâché pumpkin out of the box. It had holes for the arms, legs, and head, and stuffed inside was the sweat suit Mom had dyed orange to match.

"This is perfect," I whispered when I squeezed into the big orange ball. "All I have to do is use a black marker to put on some lines, and I'll look exactly like a walking, talking basketball! Talk about *hoop*-la!"

I managed to keep my secret all week, although Funny badgered the living daylights out of me. I didn't let on that I understood how she felt, because I was determined to march into the media center in costume for the taping on Friday afternoon and knock everybody's socks off.

As soon as the dismissal bell rang Friday, I headed for the girls' rest room, where Mom was waiting with the giant pumpkin wrapped in an old sheet. I unwrapped it and stood back to admire my handiwork. The black lines exactly matched the ones on our basketball at home. I threw on the sweat suit, and Mom helped me into the papier-mâché ball.

"Oh, Mom, you're a doll!" I cried, reaching around the big ball to hug her with my fingertips. "Look at this. I can even bounce!" I hopped up and down a couple of times, almost letting the ball touch the floor on the downward motion. "Now don't I look like a real basketball?"

Mom shook her head in amazement and chuckled. "Sometimes I wonder about you, sweetheart."

I took a deep breath and opened the door to the production room a few minutes later. Nobody noticed me at first. Then Funny glanced up, blinked in disbelief, and let out a shriek.

"Oh, my gosh, Beth! What do you think you're doing?"

The rest of the crew looked up then, and their mouths dropped open in unison.

"I'm a basketball!" I announced as I skipped into the room. "And look—I can even bounce!" With that, I dribbled myself across the floor and waited for the applause to begin.

"She *is* a basketball," cried Shawnie.

"You've got to be kidding," groaned Funny, burying her face in her hands. "You're supposed to be a co-anchor this month! You can't sit there on camera looking like a . . . a . . . a *basketball*!"

Shane gave me a lopsided grin. "Bizarre, Barry. *Totally* bizarre."

"And extremely clever," said Mr. Levine, walking forward from where he'd been consulting with Tim, this month's cameraman.

"I agree," said Shane. He came closer and inspected the costume, running a finger along one of the black lines. "Bizarre, but extremely clever."

"And there's no doubt about it, she'll have everyone at Wakeman talking about the basketball tournament," observed Mr. Levine. "Great job, Beth."

I tried not to look smug. As far as I could see, Funny was the only one with any objection to my fantastic costume. She had to know by now that she was overruled. Except she didn't.

"But bouncing?" Funny argued. "We can't have

her bouncing up and down in front of the camera. There's no telling what it would look like on the screen."

"Yeah," agreed Jon, "and half the audience might get motion sickness."

"Okay, so I won't bounce," I snapped angrily. "Will that make you happy?"

"Three minutes," Tim called out.

Funny looked totally flustered. "But we don't have a script for *a basketball*. What are you going to say, Beth?"

"Trust me," I muttered between clenched teeth.

Funny let out an exasperated breath. "I guess we'll *have* to trust you. We don't have time to come up with something else. Places, everybody." Then, firing me a warning look, she added, "But no bouncing!"

"Beth, you are an absolute scream," whispered Shawnie as we took our places on the set.

The red light on Tim's camera winked on, and Funny started the theme music. After a few seconds she lowered the volume, and Tim swung the camera to the set, where Shawnie and I waited for our cue. Sitting in a chair in the round papier-mâché costume wasn't exactly easy, and I had to bite the insides of my mouth to keep from bursting out laughing.

When the music faded out completely, Shawnie smiled into the camera and said, "Good morning, and welcome to this edition of *The Wakeman Bulletin Board*."

"We have a *very* special show for you today," I said. "We're dedicating the program to our own Wakeman Warriors and wishing them luck in the countywide basketball tournament next week. Go, Wakeman Warriors!"

"Yea, Warriors! Go, Warriors!" yelled the rest of the crew on the set.

Beaming into the camera, I stood up and turned slowly around, letting the audience get the full effect of my costume. I heard a few kids on the set giggling. They were eating it up. Funny had been stupid not to like it.

I toyed with an idea for a second. Should I? I was dying to do it. But Funny would kill me!

Who cares? Do it, anyway! the imp in me urged.

With a triumphant grin I bounced across the set.

The Fabulous Five usually gathered at my house on Saturday mornings to watch the program, but this week Alicia, Brittany, and Todd all had the flu, and Mom decided they were probably contagious. Later I talked to Katie, Jana, and Melanie on the phone, and they all raved about my costume and even congratulated me for having the nerve to wear it. So I wasn't quite prepared for what I heard when I ducked into the girls' rest room before classes Monday morning.

"That Beth Barry is totally off the wall," came a voice I didn't recognize. I frowned as the girl went on, "Did you see her on *The Wakeman Bulletin Board* Saturday morning?"

"Did I ever! Can you imagine parading around in front of a television camera looking like a giant basketball?"

"Yeah, and could you believe it, she actually *bounced*!" chimed in a third girl.

Then they broke up laughing.

I sank against the stall door, mortified, but I couldn't stop myself from listening.

"Talk about making an idiot of yourself," one of them said. "Can you imagine how embarrassed her friends must be?"

"The Fabulous Five? All I've got to say is they must be awfully loyal. It has to be tough sticking by a kook like Beth Barry."

I heard the door open and the three girls leave the rest room, but I didn't budge from the stall. I couldn't. The girls' words were still ringing in my ears. *Totally off the wall. Talk about making an idiot of yourself. Can you imagine how embarrassed her friends must be? It has to be tough sticking by a kook like Beth Barry.*

I sighed heavily. Had they been right? Had I finally gone too far and made a total idiot of myself? Worst of all, was it possible that I had embarrassed my friends?

Of course not! another part of my brain replied. I'm an actress, and everybody knows I like to do dramatic things. Be theatrical. Have fun. What was the matter with those girls, anyway? They're probably the most boring people in the world. Besides, my friends said they loved my costume. But did they? Were they lying to keep from hurting my feelings?

I tried to brush the girls' words out of my mind as I left the rest room and headed for my homeroom. The first bell had already rung, and the halls were almost deserted. But as I hurried along, I remembered the looks on everybody's faces when I bounced into the production room Friday afternoon and announced that I was a basketball.

My shoulders sagged at the memory. Funny had gone berserk, and everyone else had stared at me as if I had lost my mind. Even Shane had called me bizarre. Shane Arrington, who had hippie parents and an iguana for a pet!

Dekeisha Adams didn't help things one bit, either. In the hall between second and third periods she came bounding up to me and yelled, "Hey, Barry, what's big and round and orange and bounces? Beth Basketball!"

I felt the color drain out of my face.

"Hey, get it?" asked Dekeisha between giggles. "What's big and round and—"

"Yeah, yeah, I get it," I grumbled, and hurried away.

By lunchtime I had made up my mind to talk to

my friends again. "Did you guys really like my basketball costume?" I demanded the minute everybody was seated at our regular table.

Jana and Melanie looked at each other and burst out laughing.

"Oh, Beth, you're going to hate me," said Melanie, giggling again, "but when the show first came on, I thought you were a pumpkin!"

I felt heat creeping up my neck. It was incredible. They were just like Shane. They thought I was bizarre.

"So did I," admitted Jana. "And I couldn't figure out why you were dressed like a pumpkin. I mean, this is March, not Halloween."

"Couldn't you see the black lines?" I asked. "I drew them just like the ones on Brian and Todd's basketball."

"Yeah, that's what gave us our first clue that you weren't a pumpkin," said Katie, chuckling.

"Or an orange," added Jana. "Where was your costume when Christie was running for class president and giving away oranges? Can you imagine what you could have done for her campaign if you had come to school dressed as an orange?"

They were laughing again, and I wanted more than anything for the whole conversation to end. Those girls in the rest room were right. I had made a fool of myself.

We were almost finished eating when Alexis Duvall, Sara Sawyer, and Lisa Snow stopped by the table, all grinning from ear to ear.

"Hey, do you know who's got more bounce to the ounce?" called out Sara. "Beth Barry!"

"Yeah, and did you hear that Beth has an offer from the NBA?" asked Alexis. "They want her to pose as their official basketball!"

"That's not all," said Lisa. "The Harlem Globetrotters were interested in her, too, but it turns out she's too big, even for their hands."

I was the only one at the table who wasn't laughing.

By the end of the day, my self-confidence had plummeted. I felt like soda that had lost its fizz. Oh, there were a few kids who said how clever they thought my basketball costume had been, but most teased me or made jokes about it. "How could I have been so stupid?" I asked myself when I sat down to do my homework after dinner. "So ridiculous? So immature?"

Naturally I couldn't concentrate on homework, and after a while I closed my book and flopped down on my bed, staring at the ceiling and wondering how I could have missed seeing it. My friends had just been putting up with me. That was all there was to it. They'd been humoring me. Sticking with me because they were loyal and didn't want to hurt my feelings. It was perfectly obvious, now that I thought about it. The girls in the rest room had said the very things my own friends had been too kind to say. And wasn't I teased by some of my other friends? Dekeisha had even called me Beth Basketball!

There was only one thing to do, and I knew instantly what that was. I would have to change my entire personality. It was that simple. Since it was my kooky behavior that was causing all the problems, I would have to become a totally new and different person. I sat up in bed and reached for pencil and paper. I would make a list of all the traits I admired most in other people. Of course I would start with my friends. I would become a quiet person like Jana. Someone who was conservative and level-headed like Christie. A deep thinker like Katie. A sweet, tender person like Melanie.

I scratched my head with my pencil and lapsed into thought. Finally I began to write again. I would be kind to animals like Mona Vaughn was, sincere like Randy Kirwan, cool and laid back like Shane, a leader like Curtis Trowbridge, smiley and cheerful like Funny Hawthorne, a brilliant student like Whitney Larkin. And above all, someone who kept her mouth shut and all her crazy ideas to herself!

I started to put my list on my desk when another thought occurred to me. Maybe I should make a second list and put down all the personality traits I wanted to avoid. I didn't have to put down loud, kooky, dramatic, or flamboyant. I already had those burned into my brain. But what about gossipy like Tammy Lucero, domineering like Laura McCall, and rude and inconsiderate like Clarence Marshall?

I looked the two lists over. Wow, I thought. If I can do all this, I'll be practically perfect!

Next I dragged myself off the bed and went to my closet. What on earth could the *new me* possibly wear to school tomorrow? Loud colors and outlandish patterns almost jumped off the hangers at me. I sighed miserably, thinking about how much I loved my wardrobe, my jewelry. Eeek! My *haircut*!

Horrified, I ran to the mirror and ran my fingers through my short, spiky hair. I worked like crazy to get it to point every which way from my head. But now my favorite hairdo would have to go.

I trudged to the bathroom and dug around in the cabinet until I found my sister Brittany's mousse. Then I dunked my head in a basin of water, towel-dried my hair, and began plastering it down with the mousse.

"Oh, no! I look like a nerd!" I moaned, studying the sad face in the mirror. "Not to mention dull and boring."

Next I used my blow dryer and then plugged in Brittany's curling iron. Maybe curls were the answer. They certainly couldn't make things any worse.

The back of my hair was too short to wrap around the curling iron, but the top and sides were easy to curl. Brushing it out a few minutes later, I looked critically into the mirror.

"Gross," I murmured. "But if that's what it takes, that's what I'll do."

With my hairstyle settled, I headed back to my closet. Was there anything in there that would fit my new image? I wondered as I stared at the blazing array of colors. Of course not.

"What I need is something dull, like gray, or black, or puce. Puce would really do it. It even sounds like a dorky color." Poking a finger in my mouth, I pretended to gag.

Brittany! I thought in a flash. She has lousy taste. I tiptoed into the hall and listened at my sister's door. I didn't hear anything, so I rushed in and began going through the incredibly dull things in her closet. What I finally decided on was a pair of fawn-color stirrup pants and a chocolate brown crushed-velvet turtleneck. Praying she wouldn't miss them, I tucked them under my arm and headed back to my room. A flash of red reminded me that my fingernail polish would have to go, too.

"Beige and brown, how dull can you get?" I mumbled the next morning when I got ready for school. I was tempted for a moment to grab some gaudy jewelry to add a little life to my outfit, but instead I wore only the gold posts that had been put into my ears when I'd had them pierced last year. They were so small that they were barely noticeable. Sighing, I picked up my books, trying not to look at my dull, colorless nails, and headed for school.

"I'm going to be as quiet as Jana, as conservative as Christie, as concerned about important issues as Katie, and as sweet and tender as Melanie," I reminded myself as I hung my jacket in my locker and got out books for my morning classes. "And as kind to animals as Mona, and as sincere as Randy, and as cool and laid back as Shane, and . . ."

Just then Jana approached her locker, which was next to mine. She smiled at me and then began working her combination without a word. Suddenly she blinked and looked at me again, her expression registering total astonishment.

See a ghost? I wanted to ask, but I didn't. Instead I pretended I was Melanie. I smiled sweetly and said, "Hi, Jana."

"Beth? Is that you?" Jana blurted out.

Who were you expecting, the Tooth Fairy? I sealed my lips to keep the words inside. To really change, I would have to stop talking like the old Beth, as well as stop dressing like her.

"Of course it's me. I just changed my hair, that's all."

Jana nodded, but she seemed uncertain. "Looks nice." Then she peered closer at me and frowned. "I thought you hated curly hair."

I shrugged and thought fast. "I decided it makes me look older," I lied.

"Oh," Jana murmured, closing her locker, and we headed down the hall.

I was aware of several girls looking at me as I went past, but I pretended not to notice. I hoped they were thinking that I looked more subdued, more quiet and conservative, than the old Beth Barry.

We rounded a corner and caught up with Melanie on her way to class. We walked for several minutes, and I was so proud of myself, I wanted to jump up and down. I didn't open my mouth once!

"Gosh, you seem awfully quiet this morning," observed Melanie.

I don't want to embarrass you anymore by being a total motor mouth. I smiled at Melanie the same way Funny would smile. "Really?" I asked innocently.

Melanie looked confused, but we had reached the door to her homeroom. "See you guys at lunch," she said.

"You seem quiet to me, too," Jana told me. "Are you okay?"

No, I'm not okay. I look like a dork, and I feel like a jerk! "Sure." I spoke softly. "I'm fine . . . I just have a lot on my mind," I added, trying to imitate the concern that I always heard in Katie's voice when she was involved in one of her causes.

Jana paused at the door to her homeroom. She looked worried, but she didn't ask any more questions. "See you."

I was pleased with myself. I knew my friends would have to adjust to my new personality, but that was okay. Once they did, they would be a whole lot happier about being my friend.

I didn't hear much of anything that went on in my morning classes. I was too busy getting my self-improvement project organized. I had brought some three-by-five cards to school with me, and I sat in class making notes on them about things I wanted to remember to do. I planned to whip out the cards before I entered a room or joined a group of kids so that I would be reminded to smile and say hello to everyone, or show leadership qualities, or be a good listener. Things like that. I was impressed with myself already, and I hadn't even tried it yet.

When lunchtime came, I stuffed the cards into my purse and headed for the cafeteria. I hadn't brought my lunch today because I had avoided going into the kitchen this morning, where Brittany would spot me in her clothes and throw a fit. I stopped outside the lunchroom and shuffled through the cards one more time. I read each item quickly, trying to commit it to memory, and then got in the hot-lunch line.

My insides were churning when I reached the table where Jana, Katie, and Melanie were already seated, but I reminded myself that I had to be cool and laid back like Shane. I pretended not to notice that they had their heads together in deep conversation. I took a breath to calm myself, remembering the three-by-five card that said, "When joining a group, greet each person individually," and slid my hot-lunch tray onto the table.

"Hi, Jana. Hi, Melanie. Hi, Katie. What's up?" I asked as casually as I could.

Melanie jumped as if she'd been stuck by a pin, and Jana and Katie looked equally startled.

"Oh . . . hi," fumbled Melanie.

"Yeah, hi," said Katie. "Um, sit down."

I chuckled to myself. My plan was already working. They were obviously talking about the new me. Well, I thought, they haven't seen anything yet.

Nonchalantly I picked up my taco and took a bite. Then I opened my math book and began skimming the assignment. I knew my friends would be surprised, but it was time they realized what a brilliant student I intended to become. Besides, sometimes Christie used to read while The Fab Five were together. There was total silence at the table, but I could feel all three of them looking at me.

I hoped that the studious look on my face would give them a clue, but just in case it didn't, I announced, "I'm planning to ace that big math test next week."

I kept my eyes glued to the book, so I couldn't see if they were exchanging confused glances again, but I knew they were.

We all ate in silence for a while, until Melanie

piped up, "Would you look at that Laura McCall. She just cut into the front of the hot-lunch line, and now she's motioning for Tammy to come with her."

"Yeah, look at that," said Katie. "The kids she cut in front of are steaming, but she's refusing to move."

I peered over the top of my math book, and when I saw Laura whipping her long braid over her shoulder and sticking her nose in the air, my blood started to boil. She could make me mad faster than anyone else I knew.

I opened my mouth and was about to make a nasty remark when all of a sudden I stopped. The image of my lists loomed in my mind, and the words *sincere* and *fair-minded* sprang out from the others. If those were ways I wanted my friends to see me, I would have to bite my tongue. I would even have to say something nice about my enemy. All I hoped was that I could get through it without choking.

"Maybe Laura has a legitimate reason for cutting in line," I said, trying to sound serious, the way Katie did when she talked about her responsibility on Teen Court. When I didn't choke on those words, I kept going. "For all we know, she might be in a hurry because she has an appointment with Mr. Bell or one of her teachers during lunch period."

Jana's mouth dropped open so far, her chin almost hit the table. "Since when did you start sticking up for Laura?"

Imitating Randy, I gave her my sincere look, and said, "I was only trying to be fair." Then I buried my nose in my math book again before she could argue.

I was a nervous wreck by the time lunch period was finally over. Being perfect was exhausting. I dragged myself along the hall to English class, hoping Miss Dickinson would give us a reading assignment so that I could take a little nap. Just as I passed the biology room, I saw Shane coming toward me, looking cool as usual.

When he saw me, he stopped and began to grin. "Hey, Barry. Have you heard the news?"

I shook my head.

"You mean Mr. Bell hasn't talked to you yet? Well, he's going to. Mr. Levine, the coaches, and the whole basketball team asked him to make you Wakeman's official mascot for the basketball tournament." Shane hooked his thumbs under his arms and began to strut around the hall. "I can just see you now—Beth Basketball!—official mascot of Wakeman Junior High!"

My knees turned to Silly Putty. "Oh, no!" I groaned.

"What do you mean, oh, no? You're going to do it, aren't you? It's your kind of thing."

I mumbled something and hurried on down the hall to my class. There was no way I could explain to Shane why I could never put on that hideous orange costume again. That it belonged to the old Beth. The Beth who always made an idiot of herself. *The Beth who embarrassed her friends.*

When I walked into English class, Miss Dickinson called me to her desk. "Mr. Bell wants you to stop by his office after school," she said. Giving me a twinkling smile, she added, "Don't worry. You aren't in trouble."

Smiling weakly, I said thanks and went to my seat. I had until the end of the day to think of an excuse to give Mr. Bell for not being Wakeman's stupid, dumb, off-the-wall mascot. I slouched down as far as I could and hid behind my book, trying not to think about how great it would feel to run out onto the gym floor to the applause of the crowd. Or maybe I'd dribble across the floor like a bouncing basketball and take a big bow. Any other time I would have jumped at the chance.

"But not this time!" I told myself stubbornly. I must have said it out loud, because Joel Murphy, sitting in front of me, turned around and gave me a funny look.

I bit my lip and tried to stop thinking about being the school mascot and concentrate on the new me instead. I had plans to make. How was I going to show everybody that I was kind to animals, the way Mona was? Everybody knew I had an Old English sheepdog named Agatha, but there was no way I could bring her to school and demonstrate how kind

I was. And what was I going to wear tomorrow to make everyone think I was as conservative as Christie? I didn't dare raid Brittany's closet again. She was going to kill me as it was.

My mind was reeling by the time school ended for the day, and I wasn't any closer to a solution than I had been before.

"Come right on in, Beth, and have a seat," said Mr. Bell when Miss Simone, the school secretary, sent me into his office.

"Everybody I've spoken with is so excited about your being our mascot for the basketball tournament," he began instantly. "That costume of yours is fantastic, and it will show up terrifically on TV. Did you know that television stations from all over the tournament area will be covering the games?"

I could feel my eyes getting wide. "Television stations?" I whispered. "From all over the county?" For a second I wanted to leap up and shout. This was my big opportunity to become a *real* television star. But my throat tightened as I remembered that the new Beth Barry would never think of making such an idiot of herself and risk humiliating her best friends in the whole world.

"That's right," Mr. Bell said, beaming. "And I've talked to our band director about working up a special fight song just for your routine. And of course you're already a cheerleader, so you can jump into step with them, too. Isn't it exciting? You're going to be one of the biggest stars of the tournament!"

I swallowed hard and blinked back tears. "I'm . . . I'm . . ." I tried to say "I'm sorry," but the words wouldn't come. How was I going to turn down a chance like this? I clutched my purse. Why didn't I have a three-by-five card that would tell me what to do?

"Is something wrong?" Mr. Bell asked kindly.

"I just can't do it," I blurted out. My heart was bursting. I fumbled around for some way to explain and finally said, "My parents won't let me go out on school nights, and the tournament starts Wednesday."

I looked straight at the floor, agonizing while I waited for his reply.

"I see," he said slowly. "And I don't suppose they would make an exception this time?"

I shook my head vigorously. "I *know* they wouldn't."

"Well, that's too bad, Beth," said Mr. Bell. "But why don't you talk to your parents . . . just in case?"

"Okay," I agreed in a small voice. I said good-bye and left his office, wishing that I had never set eyes on that papier-mâché pumpkin. And that I had never painted black lines on it to make it look like a basketball or worn it on *The Wakeman Bulletin Board*. Because then I wouldn't have made a fool of myself, and I wouldn't have to turn down the chance to appear on *real* TV.

You mean, make a fool of yourself on *real* TV, grumbled another part of my brain.

The halls were practically deserted as I headed toward my locker, but when I rounded the last corner, I saw that Jana, Katie, and Melanie were still there, and it looked as if they were waiting for me.

"Hurry up, slow poke, we're going to Bumpers," called Melanie when I got closer.

"Yeah. Where have you been?" asked Katie. "The bell rang ages ago."

I wanted to break down and tell them the awful truth, that I had been to see Mr. Bell and turned down my big chance to be on television. I wanted to tell them that I was tired of pretending I was somebody I wasn't and that I wanted to go back to being the old Beth Barry instead of the fake new me. But of course I couldn't. I was doing all this for them. So that they could *really* like me and wouldn't have to be embarrassed about being my friend anymore.

But what could I say? I couldn't pull out my three-by-five cards in front of them. Then I remembered my lists. Mentally I went down the line and stopped at Whitney Larkin. What would Whitney say at a moment like this? Calmly I looked at my friends and said, "Gee, I'd love to, guys, but I really have to study. I'm determined to ace that math test, so I guess you'll just have to go on without me."

It was obvious my friends didn't know what to say, so they nodded and murmured good-bye and left me alone at my locker. As soon as they were gone, I threw open the door, grabbed my jacket, and hurried home—where I could cry.

I was stretched across my bed a little while later, sobbing my heart out, when I heard the doorbell ring. For once in my life I was the only one home, except for Agatha, who was barking up a storm. I raised my head off the pillow and listened, hoping whoever it was would go away. It's probably some little kid selling candy for the Cub Scouts.

It rang again, and the instant the sound died away, I heard Agatha thundering up the stairs. She bounded into my room and barked furiously at me, insisting in her own way that I get up and answer the door.

"Go away, Agatha," I mumbled as I dried my eyes.

But Agatha wasn't going anywhere until I answered the door. She trotted over to the bed and stood so close that I could feel her hot breath on my face when she barked.

This time whoever was at the door leaned against the bell. It bonged over and over again until I couldn't stand it anymore.

"Okay! Okay!" I shouted. I headed out of my room, glancing into the mirror as I went past. The face I saw was red and puffy. I couldn't believe how awful I looked. It had better just be some little kid at the door, I thought.

"I'm coming!" I yelled. I turned the lock by the knob, but left the chain lock secured so that I could peer out and see who was there before completely opening the door. My eyes nearly popped out of my head when I saw the three faces looking back at me.

"We're calling a special meeting of The Fab Five," said Jana. Beside her, Melanie and Katie were nodding solemnly.

"Come on, open the door," urged Katie.

I blew out a big breath and tried frantically to decide what to do. I couldn't let them see me this way. I looked as if I'd been run over by a truck!

"Just a minute," I called out. Slamming the door, I raced to the bathroom off the kitchen and splashed cold water on my face. I blew my nose and ran my fingers through my hair. One side was still curly, but the other side drooped into my eyes. "I'm a mess!" I whispered.

My friends were leaning on the doorbell again, which naturally set Agatha off. She was pawing at the door and barking at the top of her lungs.

Hurrying back, I slipped the chain lock and let in my friends, following them as they charged straight into the family room and arranged themselves stiffly on the sofa and chairs. I didn't like what was happening. They looked mad, or at least upset.

"What's the emergency?" I asked weakly.

They exchanged frowns and then turned to me and said in unison, "You."

I gulped. "Me?"

"If you don't want to be in The Fabulous Five anymore, why don't you just come out and tell us?" demanded Katie.

"We thought we were your best friends," Jana said sadly.

"But . . . but . . ." I spluttered. I was flabbergasted. I couldn't understand what they were talking about.

"We couldn't believe how different you were acting today," said Melanie. "First it was your clothes and your hair."

"Then you didn't even *sound* like your old self," continued Katie. She narrowed her eyes accusingly. "And since when did you start using your grades as an excuse to avoid being with your friends?"

"But we really knew something was wrong when you started sticking up for Laura McCall," said Jana. "You used to loathe the very ground she walked on, but all of a sudden you were making excuses for her rotten behavior."

Melanie shook her head. "That wasn't one bit like you."

"Nothing you did today was like you," added Jana. "The whole school is buzzing about it."

"We talked it over, and all we could think of was that you're planning to drop out of The Fabulous

Five," said Katie, "and join The Fantastic Four-some."

"So we've come here to tell you how hurt we are that you don't like us anymore," murmured Jana, "and ask you what we can do to stay your friends."

I was so stunned that I couldn't say anything for a moment. I just stared at them through watery eyes.

"I don't . . . I mean . . . you thought . . ." I threw up my hands in frustration. "You don't understand!" I cried. "It's *because* I like you that I'm trying to change!"

I cleared my throat and started telling them about the three girls in the bathroom. "They said I embarrassed you and that you hung around with me only to be loyal," I said between sobs.

"Oh, Beth," Jana cried, running to me and putting her arms around me. "How could you believe a thing like that?"

"Especially when you didn't even know the girls who said it," said Melanie.

"And they don't know the first thing about The Fabulous Five," pointed out Katie.

"That's what I thought, too, at first," I admitted. I went on to remind them of how they'd thought my costume was bizarre when they first saw me on *The Wakeman Bulletin Board*, and how Dekeisha had teased me, even calling me Beth Basketball, and how Lisa, Alexis, and Sara had made jokes. "It all started to add up, and pretty soon I was convinced that I had made a colossal fool of myself. Not only that, I had made you look foolish, too, for being my friends."

We talked for a while longer, and I told them about my self-improvement campaign. I even showed them my three-by-five cards.

"Forget those," Jana told me, glancing at the cards and pitching them back to me. "We love you just the way you are."

"Do you really mean that?" I asked. "I mean, you don't think the *new me* is really a better person?"

"Never," declared Katie. "I actually missed your being off the wall. It just didn't feel normal with you walking around acting intelligent and polite and *quiet*."

I grabbed a pillow off the sofa and threw it at Katie. It missed because she ducked, and we all started to giggle.

"What a relief," I said with a big sigh. Suddenly I sat up straight. Something wonderful had just occurred to me. I held up my hand for quiet.

"Now you really mean what you said, don't you?" I asked. "You really want the old Beth Barry back?"

"Of course," they replied in unison.

I ran to the phone and looked up Mr. Bell's home phone number in the book. After I had punched in the number and was listening to it ring, I turned to my friends and said, "Then I know you won't mind

that I'm calling Mr. Bell right now to tell him I *can*
wear my basketball costume and be Wakeman's mascot for the tournament starting Wednesday night."

"What!" shrieked Katie. "Not again!"

I giggled. "It's going to be on television, too, and
this time it's *real* TV, seen all over the county."

Just then Mr. Bell said hello, and I told him the
great news.

When we hung up, I did a cartwheel across the
floor. Then I turned to my friends and grinned.
"What you see is what you get," I said impishly.

They started grinning, too. We all raised our fists
into the air and shouted, "The Fab Five forever!
The Fab Five forever!" until we dropped from exhaustion.

I still don't know who the three girls in the bathroom
were, but in a way I'm glad that I overheard their
conversation. Because of them, I've learned to appreciate my friends more than ever, and they appreciate me, too. And the picture on page 197 of
The Wigwam—the one of Beth Basketball bouncing
around the gym floor with the crowd going wild—
will always be one of my favorite memories of Wakeman Junior High.

CHAPTER

6

*A*fter Mr. Bell had presented the last award and recognized the last club, a cheer went up. Crazy Reggie put on a fast song and turned up the volume. Music blared from the speakers, and couples started pouring onto the dance floor.

"I can't believe that this year is really over," Jana shouted to her friends over the music.

"Me, either," Melanie replied sadly. "So much has happened."

"Yeah. You met me," said Shane, grinning impishly.

"And Igor," Melanie reminded him. "Don't forget him. Why isn't he here tonight?"

"He wanted to come, but couldn't find a date," answered Shane.

"If only I'd known!" cried Beth. "Igor and I could have come together."

Everyone laughed at that, and then Beth turned serious. "Remember when we first came to Wakeman in September?" They all nodded. "We were so worried about meeting all the new kids from the other schools."

"That's true," said Katie. "And just look at how terrific *some* of them turned out to be." She nudged Tony and gave him a big smile.

"We've made lots of new friends," commented Melanie, "like Dekeisha and Shawnie..."

"And Funny," added Jana. "But I remember that when I first became friends with her, you guys thought I was a traitor."

Katie shrugged. "A lot's changed since then." She looked thoughtful for a moment. "I guess next year we'll meet a whole new set of kids, you know, the ones who'll be coming to Wakeman because of redistricting. Does anybody know yet which school they'll be coming from?"

"I heard it might be Grover," said Tony.

Beth's eyebrows shot up. "Grover! That school's in the roughest part of town."

"Right," chimed in Jana. "I'd be afraid to walk down some of those streets in broad daylight. Why would they send those kids here, anyway?"

"Oh, come on," said Katie. "That's just a rumor. Besides, even if they do come here, we should give them a chance."

"You're right, as usual, Katie," Melanie told her, smiling.

Suddenly Randy changed the subject. "Let's dance," he suggested, taking Jana's hand.

She smiled at him and followed him onto the dance floor.

"Well, I'll tell you one thing that isn't going to change," he said, beaming down at her as they danced to a slow song.

"What's that?" asked Jana.

"You and me. It doesn't matter who comes to Wakeman or what anybody else does. We'll still be together," Randy whispered.

Jana smiled at him. "Yeah, and no more experiments with dating other people. Just you and me."

Across the dance floor Melanie swayed to the beat with Shane. She was so happy, she thought she would explode. She had the most fabulous friends in the world *and* the greatest boyfriend. She chuckled to herself. She had thought she would die laughing when Mr. Bell had read aloud from the section in the yearbook where Shane and Igor had listed their top five reasons why this year had been totally cool.

She had her own reasons for believing the past year had been cool. Besides meeting Shane, she had been on the cheerleading squad, and she and her friends had saved some animals at the shelter from being put to sleep on Christmas Eve. And then there were all the great times they'd had hanging out at Bumpers. Would all that change next year? Would the new kids from Grover try to invade Bumpers?

Don't worry about it, she thought. You'll still have Shane and The Fabulous Five and a whole new year to look forward to. She had promised herself that she would try really hard to stay out of trouble next year. But you never know, she admitted to herself, smiling. Anything can happen.

Shane cocked his head. "Hey, what's so funny?"

Melanie grinned mysteriously. "I'll never tell."

Katie sat holding Tony's hand, watching everyone dance, as Tony talked to Bill Soliday. On the table in front of her was the yearbook. She glanced at it, tracing the words *Wakeman Junior High* on its cover.

A whole year had been captured here. Well, not everything's here, she thought, or else it would be too huge to pick up. There's nothing in the yearbook about my time capsule project, and thank goodness there's nothing about the trouble my going into the boys' bathroom caused!

"Hey, Katie," called Daphne Alexandrou. She and Shelly Bramlett were coming toward the table. "Will you sign our yearbooks?"

"Sure, if you'll sign mine," replied Katie.

The girls exchanged signatures, and then Katie said, "I wonder if Mr. Bell will let us have a Teen

Court again next year. If he does, I don't know who could possibly take your places as judges."

"We'll miss you, too," said Shelly. "We'll try to get a Teen Court started in high school and save you a place. Okay?"

Katie nodded and watched the two girls move on to another table. Now that the pages of this yearbook were filled, she and her friends would begin having experiences that would fill next year's yearbook.

Suddenly an idea popped into Katie's mind, and she looked at the stud earring in Tony's ear. *What an opportunity*, she thought.

Her eyes narrowed as she considered the possibilities that lay ahead. Next year we're going to have a whole new school, and it'll be a great chance for us students to make it a good one. If we start planning now, we can get some dumb rules changed, like the one about boys' not being allowed to wear earrings.

"Tony," she said, yanking on his jacket sleeve, "I've got to talk to you. When we leave here tonight, we've got to get everyone together at Bumpers for a meeting about changing some school rules next year."

Tony grinned. "Uh-oh, Your Honor. Here we go again."

Beth stood at the edge of the dance floor with Dekeisha and Marcie, talking and watching the couples dance.

"I'm really going to miss you guys," she said. "I can't believe you're both going to be gone all summer and I won't see either of you until September. It's going to be awful."

"I know," agreed Dekeisha, sighing. "But my parents think that spending the summer with my cousin in San Francisco is the greatest thing I could do. They say traveling is educational."

"I'm going to summer camp in Wisconsin," said Marcie. "This will be the fifth year I've gone, and believe me, I'd rather stay here. You've got to write and tell me *everything* that happens while I'm gone."

"Me, too," added Dekeisha. "Promise?"

"Sure," replied Beth.

Crazy Reggie was playing one of her favorite songs, and she rocked with the beat. As much as she liked being with Dekeisha and Marcie, she wished she were dancing with a boy. But Keith Masterson, the boy she had gone steady with until recently, was with Lisa Snow, and no one else was around.

Just then Heather Clark walked up with a boy Beth hadn't seen at Wakeman before. He was tall, dark-haired, and good-looking, and Beth felt her heart skip a beat when he gave her a cocky smile.

"Hi," Heather greeted them. "I want you guys to meet my cousin, Danny Engels, from New York. His family's moving to town, and he'll be in our grade at Wakeman next year. Danny, this is Beth, Marcie, and Dekeisha."

As Heather talked, Beth found she couldn't pull her eyes away from Danny, and to her surprise he seemed to be looking at her, too.

Marcie moved closer to Danny and said, "Hi. Welcome to Wacko Middle School."

Ignoring Marcie, Danny looked straight at Beth. "Want to dance?" he asked.

Little tingles raced up and down Beth's spine. "Sure."

Maybe next year will be a good one after all, she thought as she followed Danny out onto the dance floor.

By the time Beth and Danny started dancing, Christie had fallen back asleep, but now she was dreaming about the Wakeman dinner-dance. She was there with all of her friends—The Fabulous Five, plus her British friends.

Suddenly Chase and Connie appeared from out of nowhere and stood nose-to-nose, glaring at each other. She tried to tell them not to be angry with each other, but they didn't seem to hear her. Then both boys beckoned to her, and she didn't know which one to go to. How could she choose? She liked them both! Christie groaned, and tossed in her sleep. When she got home in a few weeks, not everything was going to be easy.

* * *

At eleven o'clock Crazy Reggie played one last song. Then the laser lights and light-sticks were turned off, the gymnasium lights came on, and all the students started gathering their things.

Outside the entrance to the gym, kids hung around, talking and saying good-bye, not wanting to leave. Others shouted things like "Have a great summer" as they got into their parents' cars. Jana and Randy, Katie and Tony, Melanie and Shane, and Beth lingered until almost everyone had gone.

Finally Melanie turned to the others. Tears glistened in her eyes. "I'm going to miss everyone so much, especially the eighth graders. Won't it seem strange to be at Wacko without them?"

"I know what you mean," agreed Beth. A picture of Danny Engels flashed into her mind. "But we could meet some interesting new kids."

"Well, one thing we know for sure," offered Jana. "Christie will be back, and The Fabulous Five will be together again."

"Yeah," said Katie. "And when we're together, nothing can stop us."

Jana held her yearbook in the air. "I propose a pledge. The FAB 5 FOREVER!" she called.

The others held their yearbooks up, too.

"The *FAB 5 FOREVER*!" they shouted in unison.

"The best is yet to come!" yelled Melanie.

Then, in unison again, they cried, "*THE BEST IS YET TO COME!*"

WAKEMAN JUNIOR HIGH

YEARBOOK

THE WIGWAM

I'll never forget hanging out at bumpers after school. It's a great place to see and be seen! Meet you there next fall!

— Laura McCall

Laura
-n-
?

HAVE FUN IN 8TH GRADE!! Alexis Duvall

PEAK WAS LOTS OF FUN AND SO WAS DISSECTING COWS' ♡yeballs IN BIOLOGY CLASS! I'LL NEVER FORGET THE DAY THE Wacko Super Quiz team beat Trumbull!

Love, Whitney Larkin

WL + CT = ♡

There will be lots of juicy gossip next year!
Love,
Tammy Lucero

IT'S BEEN GREAT KNOWING YOU. SHIRLEY, BATMAN, ROBIN, AND I ARE FLYING OFF TO HIGH SCHOOL! SCARY THOUGHT, HUH?

PAUL SMOKE

THE MOUTH

Fantastic Foursome

Be kind to animals! Love, Mona Vaughn

Wacko is #1!

GOODLUCK IN 8th GRADE! Love, Melissa McConnell

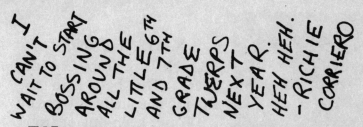
I CAN'T WAIT TO START BOSSING AROUND ALL THE LITTLE 6TH AND 7TH GRADE TWERPS NEXT YEAR. HEH HEH. —RICHIE CORRIERO

Welcome to your yearbook, fellow Wacko Warriors! For all of us at Wakeman it was a year of fun, accomplishment . . . and very big changes. Here's a look back at a very special year (and a glimpse at the one ahead)! Enjoy!

Funny Hawthorne and Jana Morgan
Seventh-Grade Coeditors

Greetings from London! I can't wait to come back to Wakeman this fall! —Christie Winchell

FAB FIVE FOREVER!

Remember the Spooky Halloween Show? Double, double, toil and 'trouble'!
Dekeisha Adams

At next year's celebrity auction, I want to bid on the Denver Broncos' football!!! —Keith Masterson

Broncos #1!

KATIE SHANNON

ERA/NOW... Fab 5 Forever... The best man for the job is usually a woman ... Tony, keep out of trouble!

BETH BARRY

Shawnie, wanna go shopping?...Cheerleaders unite! ...Dekeisha—"Double, double, toil and trouble"... Fab 5 FOREVER! ... Broadway, here I come!

JANA MORGAN

Fab 5 forever! We've come a long way, girls ... Randy, you're the best—no more "experiments." Wanna come over for pizza? ... Funny, working on the yearbook with you was great—let's do it again next year!

MELANIE EDWARDS
Go Wakeman cheerleaders ...JM, BB, CW, KS—Fab 5 Forever! ...I love The New Generation ...Shane, you're #1—except for Igor!

CHRISTIE WINCHELL
Fab 5—Friends Forever! ... Jon, thanks for being a friend ...Wakeman tennis rules ...CC—maybe my 8th-grade curfew will be later ...London's great, but Wakeman, I miss you! See you next year!

We on *The Wigwam* staff decided that it's time to turn the tables and give grades to the teachers at Wakeman. We asked kids around school to fill out a report card on some of our intellectual leaders, and here are the results:

Teacher: *Mr. Dracovitch*
Ability to make class fun: *A+*
Vampire wardrobe: *C–*
Comments: *Voted most likely to move to Transylvania (or most likely to stay here and win Teacher of the Year)!*

Teacher: *Miss Wolfe*
Physical fitness: *A*
Mercy on cheerleaders during workouts: *D*
Comments: *Vill probably coach the first American Olympic Cheerleading team!*